MAIL ORDER MAMA

BRIDES OF BECKHAM BOOK TWO

KIRSTEN OSBOURNE

UNLIMITED DREAMS

When Emily's mother decides to marry, her fiancé says that twenty year old Emily needs to find a new place to live before the wedding. Emily has always been exceedingly shy and has no idea what to do. She runs across an advertisement for mail order brides and responds, hoping to find a good situation. Benjamin lost the love of his life just months before. He and his girls need a new mama in their house. Will Emily be the mama they need?

To sign up for Kirsten Osbourne's mailing list and receive notice of new titles as they are available, click here.

CHAPTER 1

$\mathcal{M}$innesota, August 1883

BENJAMIN CAREFULLY PULLED weeds out of the ground surrounding his wife's grave. "I miss you every day. The girls miss you, and are starting to make noise about wanting a new mom." He traced her name on the tombstone. "Anna, the world was a good place when you were by my side, but now I feel like I'm surrounded by darkness. How could I ever find someone to be a new mom for our precious girls?"

He looked up at the sky, still angry with God for taking away his beautiful wife. "I think I'm going to send for a mail order bride. There's an agency out East that will send a woman out to me. I have to pay them, but I don't care. I don't really want a wife, but I do need a new mama for the girls. Abbie starts school in just a year, and she's already telling me that she needs more grown up dresses. I don't know how to dress a little girl. *Mor* helps, but she doesn't live with us, and I couldn't pull her away from *Far*. I need a woman who will live with us to be a mother to the children. I guess I don't really need a bride. I need a mail order mama to take care of our girls."

He knew he was rambling and anyone walking past the small cemetery would think he was crazy. "I feel like I'm betraying you by even considering finding a new wife, but the girls need someone." He couldn't lie to Anna, even after she was dead. "I need someone to keep me warm at night, but I won't fall in love with her, Anna. I promise you."

He laid the flowers he and the girls had picked on her grave, and walked the short distance back to the home he shared with his daughters above the mercantile he owned.

He'd gone out after work, but before he'd started supper. Abbie did a good job of watching Georgie while he worked, but she was only six, and he couldn't make himself leave them any longer, even though he could see their home from the cemetery. He had to worry twice as much now that Anna couldn't share the worries with him.

He went to the table and called the girls to him. Once they were there, he told them about his decision. "I've decided to send away for a mail order bride, so you girls can have a mama again."

Georgie hugged her father, and Abbie just nodded solemnly. Both girls resembled their parents a great deal. Benjamin and Anna were both children of Norwegian immigrants, and had the typical Norwegian build and coloring. Both had the same blond hair and blue eyes of their parents and their parents before them. Everyone had stopped and stared as he and Anna had walked along the street together. Now the girls both reminded him a great deal of his Anna. Every time he looked at them, she was on his mind.

"May we help you write the letter, Papa?" The girls didn't use the Norwegian words for mother and father, *Mor* and

Far, like he and Anna had. They knew only a few words in the old language, and that suited Benjamin fine. He'd had to learn to speak English when he'd started school, and it had been hard for him. He wanted his girls to speak the language of their new country. They would know the Norwegian words they needed to keep his mother happy, but no more. Now his parents used English more than Norwegian at home anyway.

Benjamin nodded. "After supper, we'll write the best letter a bride has ever seen." He stood up to go into the kitchen, wondering what he'd do for supper. His mother had brought over some fresh bread just that morning. Maybe he could make some sandwiches. The girls hated them, but he knew very little about cooking and even less about cleaning. If *Mor* didn't clean his house every week and do his family's laundry, he didn't know how he'd manage.

He quickly sliced the bread and fried some bacon, one of the few things he knew how to cook. He carried the bread and bacon to the table on plates along with some of his *Mor's* fresh butter. The girls came in to see what he'd set out to eat. "Bacon sandwiches again?" Georgie asked.

Abbie shook her head at her sister. "Remember, he's getting us a mama to cook for us," she whispered.

Georgie sat down at the table and buttered her bread, adding the bacon. "Thanks for cooking, Papa." The words were said begrudgingly, but they were polite, and Benjamin couldn't ask for more. He was getting tired of bacon sandwiches himself.

Abbie took her seat and made her sandwich, and then they all bowed their heads to pray. Once Benjamin was finished, Abbie started telling him all she wanted him to put in the letter. "Tell her she needs to love little girls and know how to sew a dress."

Georgie looked up at that. "Tell her she needs to like to bake and cook things other than bacon sandwiches."

"And reading stories out loud. She needs to read us stories." Abbie loved stories and couldn't wait to learn to read them for herself.

"She needs to like picnics and walking in the woods."

Benjamin laughed softly. "Why don't you girls save your ideas, and we'll write the letter just as soon as I finish up the supper dishes." He was happy the girls were so excited to have a new mama. It would help them to adjust to having a woman around.

~

MASSACHUSETTS SEPTEMBER 1883

EMILY SAT in the parlor of the small house she shared with her mother, reading through the newspaper. She needed a new job. She was a cook for a well-to-do family in town, but they'd begun having her cook, clean and watch the children for no extra pay. She loved children, and she didn't mind cleaning up the messes she made, but she was still earning her very small salary. If she was going to do extra work, her pay needed to be higher commensurate with that work.

She spotted an advertisement for mail order brides and wrinkled her nose. She wanted to marry, but wasn't sure she could agree to something like that. She was glad she didn't have to. With as shy as she was, she may never find a man to marry, though. One day, she may find herself wanting to marry badly enough she'd answer an ad like that. She was glad that day wasn't today. Her eyes moved on quickly to the next ad.

She heard the front door open and close and looked up as

her mother joined her in their parlor. It was after nine at night. Her mother had never stayed out that late, but she had gradually stayed out later and later during the time she'd been seeing her new beau, William.

"How was your evening?" she asked, noting the sparkle in her mother's eyes.

Jane held out her hand to show something to Emily. A ring. "It's beautiful, Mother." William was her mother's first beau since her father was killed in Hendersonville, North Carolina during the war. "From William?" Of course it was from William. Who else would be buying her mother rings?

Jane nodded her face pink with happiness. "He asked me to marry him."

Emily jumped to her feet and hugged her mother. "I'm so happy for you!" Emily and her mother had been everything to one another since her father had died. She was thrilled her mother had finally found a man to make her happy.

"I was a little worried you'd think he was trying to take your father's place." Jane's face was serious as she searched her daughter's.

Emily shrugged. "I don't have any memories of my father at all, so I don't mind. I'm just glad you're happy."

Jane sat down next to Emily on the small pink sofa. "There is one thing, though." Jane looked worried about whatever it was. They'd always been completely honest with one another, so Emily was surprised.

"What is it?" Emily took Jane's hand in hers to give her courage to tell her about whatever was troubling her.

Jane took a deep breath, staring down at her hands. "William wants us to be alone. He thinks it could hurt our marriage to have you living in the house with us."

Emily's eyes widened. At twenty, she'd never even had a beau. It hadn't occurred to her she would need to find a place to live anytime soon. Her heart jumped into her throat and she wanted to protest, but she looked at her mother's face and knew her happiness came first. She'd been twenty with a two year old child when her husband died, and she'd found a job and supported them both for years. "I understand. When will the wedding take place?"

"In two months. I hope it will give you enough time." Jane was obviously worried about sending her daughter away, but she wanted to marry William, and it was time she did something for herself for a change.

"I'll figure something out." Emily's mind frantically reviewed what she'd just seen in the paper. Not only would she need a better paying job, but a place to live as well. She took the paper, and stood up. "I'm going to bed. Tomorrow's a work day."

As she climbed the stairs, Emily knew she wouldn't be blowing out the light anytime soon. She'd spend the night searching for something, *anything*, she could do to support herself.

She went into her room and quickly changed into her nightgown and braided her long brunette hair before lying down on the bed with the newspaper. She quickly read through the rest of the want ads, but there were very few jobs for a woman in Beckham. It was a mid-sized town, but most of the women stayed home with their families.

Her eyes landed once again on the advertisement for a mail order bride. She read it over carefully. "Mail Order Bride agency needs women who are looking for the adventure of their lives. Men out West need women to marry. Reply in person at 300 Rock Creek Road. See Mrs. Harriett Long."

Emily bit her lip. Could she really do such a thing? It would solve a lot of her problems. She wouldn't need to get a job, and she'd have a place to live. Of course, she'd also be married to a man she'd never met. Did she really have another option, though?

∼

EMILY SPENT the day cooking with Mary and Sally, the children of the Walters, the family she worked for. The girls wanted to learn how to bake cakes, so she was once again teaching them. She couldn't help but wonder if their mother told them to ask her how to cook various things so she could get some time away and not have to hire a nurse for them.

She enjoyed having the children with her, but it did make her day harder. She fixed three meals per day for the family of four, and when the girls were with her, she tended to have to clean up more messes and do extra baking. The girls were three and five, and made more messes than she had ever dreamed possible. She would put the youngest in a chair at the table and have to help her do everything. The older girl was a little better but not by much.

At one point, halfway through the day, she looked up to see Mary, the three year old, throwing eggs on the floor. "Where did she get eggs from?" Emily asked her pointed gaze fixed on Sally.

Sally smiled and shrugged her shoulders trying to look innocent. Because Emily had no true authority over the girls, she couldn't punish them for their misdeeds, so she let it go and patiently cleaned up the mess.

Before the day was out, she'd mopped the kitchen floor six times. She was exhausted. She was also determined to stop by the address on Rock Creek Road on her way home. Being a mail order bride couldn't possibly compare to the hassle of working with the two Walters daughters. How could having her own home be worse than working with the two destructive girls?

At the end of the day, she stood in the spotless kitchen, and thanked Mrs. Walters for her wages. She was always paid on Saturdays, but her money went straight to her mother for the household expenses. How could she save up enough money to move out on her own when she had to give all her money to her mother simply to make ends meet?

On her way home, she stopped at the address on Rock Creek Road. She knew where the road was, of course, but had never been on it. The house named in the address was large and intimidating. Emily had grown up in a small home, but her mother talked about the grand house she'd lived in with her parents before the war. They'd both died during the war, but Emily had frequently daydreamed about living in their beautiful home with them.

For a moment, looking up at the house, she lost her nerve and started to walk away. She'd taken ten steps before she caught herself and turned back around, marching straight up to the door and knocking.

The door was answered by a tall dark man in a butler's uniform. "Yes?"

"I'm here to see Mrs. Harriett Long, please." She made sure her voice was strong as she asked, but it would have been so much easier to mumble. Emily hated having to speak with strangers more than just about anything in the world. She'd stayed at a bad job for two years rather than interview for something else, because she was so nervous about meeting strangers.

The man nodded and stepped aside to allow her into the home. She stared around her in awe, never having been in a home so beautiful. "Right this way, Miss?"

Emily tore her gaze from a painting on the wall to follow the butler. "Hughes. Emily Hughes." She needed to stop gawking instead of looking like she'd never seen an affluent house before, so she forced her eyes on the butler's back as she followed him through the house.

He led her down a long hallway and stopped at a doorway on the left. "Ma'am? There's a Miss Emily Hughes to see you."

Emily's first impression of Harriett was surprise a woman so young, and so obviously wealthy, would have an agency for mail order brides. Harriett couldn't be more than twenty-eight and had her blond hair pulled back in a neat bun. Her petite form was encased in a blue silk dress that Emily was sure would have cost six weeks' worth of her wages.

Harriett stood and moved across the room to where Emily stood in the hall. Emily noted her movements were graceful despite a pronounced limp. She held her hand out. "It's nice to meet you, Emily. I'm Harriett Long."

"I came about your advertisement in the paper," Emily blurted out quickly as she shook Harriett's hand.

Harriett's smile brightened her entire face and made her eyes twinkle with laughter. "I presumed as much." She turned to the butler. "Would you bring some tea and cookies, Higgins?"

"Right away, Ma'am." He left them alone, quietly closing the door behind him.

"Come and sit with me. We'll talk, and I'll see if I can find a man who would suit you." Harriett waited until Emily was seated before continuing. "What made you decide to come to me?"

Emily let out a heavy sigh. "It was never my plan to be a mail order bride." She looked into Harriett's green eyes as she spoke, finding them warm and full of laughter. "I've lived with my mother my entire life. My father was killed in the war." At Harriett's nod, she continued, determined to get the full story out. "My mother and I are extremely close, and as she never remarried, I've been working and contributing to the household income for the last three years since I finished my schooling."

"How old are you now?" Harriett pulled out a piece of paper to jot down notes on what Emily told her.

"I'm twenty." She waited until Harriett wrote something down and returned her attention to her before adding, "My mother has been seeing a man for the last several months. He's her first beau since my father died." Emily rubbed the back of her neck, the strain of the last day obvious in her stature. "Last night she came home and told me he'd asked her to marry him. I'm thrilled for her, of course. She deserves to be loved."

"Of course." Harriett watched her carefully as if she were waiting to hear why she was stating the obvious.

"But her fiancé doesn't wish to have me living in the home with them once they're married. He feels there wouldn't be enough privacy if I were there, which I understand completely, but it does leave me out in the cold." Emily tried her best not to sound hurt by the situation, but she realized she was in a way. She didn't want her mother to choose her over William, but she did want her to think she was important enough to consider.

Harriett nodded. "Yes, that's more than a bit of a bind they're leaving you in. You said you've worked for the past three years? What do you do?" Harriett seemed to be genuinely interested in Emily's answers for more than just business reasons which made her much easier to talk to than most people.

Emily let out a half laugh. "I work as a cook, but often I'm expected to clean and take care of the children of the household as well."

Harriett raised an eyebrow. "And you're paid extra for those tasks?"

"Of course not. I'm paid as a cook, nothing more."

"I see. Do you enjoy working with the children?"

Emily nodded. "I do enjoy them, but they make my job a great deal harder." She explained the messes they'd made during the long day and how many times she'd had to mop the floor. "If all I had to do was mind the children, I wouldn't mind so much, but my employer enjoys giving dinner parties. She gave one tonight, in fact. So while I was cooking for her party, I was minding the children who were destroying the kitchen."

Harriett smiled. "I suppose that would explain the flour in your hair."

Emily groaned running a hand across the top of her head, messing up her severe bun. "I should have checked my appearance before I came. I'm so sorry Mrs. Long." Emily was embarrassed to be seen by anyone with flour in her hair. She usually checked her appearance before leaving work, but she'd been in a hurry to go to Rock Creek Road and start working toward becoming a mail order bride.

"It's not a problem. If you were a wife there would be times when your husband would come home and there would be flour in your hair. You're interviewing to be a wife." She turned to the desk she was sitting in front of and quickly looked through the letters in front of her. "I put an advertisement in a few papers out West thinking I would get enough responses to place the five women I had available for marriage. I received twelve letters in response. I found one other young lady to send, but you, my dear, are a godsend." She obviously found what she was looking for and held up a letter. "I think this is the letter for you." She handed it to Emily and invited her to open it, making a few more notes as she waited for Emily to read it.

Unfolding the single page of paper, Emily read the letter. "Dear Potential Bride, I'm a single father of two daughters aged four and six. Their names are Georgie and Abbie. My wife died of scarlet fever a couple of months ago, and I admit, I'm frantic trying to keep my household together. My daughters are insisting I put several things in this letter, so here is what they require in their mail order mama. She must be able to cook more things than bacon, and must never serve a bacon sandwich for supper. She must love children, especially daughters, and enjoy reading to them at night. She must know how to sew pretty dresses and fix hair 'just so'. She must be able to smile even when her new daughters make a mess. She must like to bake and enjoy picnicking and walks in the woods. On my part, I'm looking for a wife who will be willing to take on the duties of motherhood and be a good wife. I would not dream of finding a new wife so quickly if my daughters were not so badly in need of a new mother. I would like to have a wife who would occasionally be willing to help out in the mercantile store I own here in Live Oak, Minnesota. If you think you can be all of that to three very lonely people who need a good woman in their lives, please respond. I am twenty-eight years old, and would like a woman who is at least twenty, but not more than twenty-five. My daughters and I await your response. My best, Benjamin Johnson."

Emily looked up when she was finished to find Harriett watching her. "What do you think?"

Emily nodded slowly. "They sound like the kind of family I could be content with. I think." She bit her lip considering her situation. "So what now? I just write them a letter? Do I write it through you? Do I have to pay you to help me?"

"No, you don't pay me. There's a small fee for the gentleman requesting a wife, but nothing for the bride. You write a letter here, or you go home and write a letter and bring it to me to mail. All correspondence will go through me. What's our time frame?" At Emily's blank stare, she asked, "When is your mother getting married."

"Oh! I was lost in my thoughts thinking about the Johnson family. My mother's getting married in two months, so I need to be ready to leave before then." She knew it wasn't much time and she bit her lip wondering how Mrs. Long would react to the rushed time frame.

"We can make that happen. Why don't we write your letter together, and I'll mail it off for you. So many times, women forget to include pertinent details, and they kick themselves later. I have a list of things I try to make sure every letter includes, so it would be easier to do it here. The more complete your first letter is, the faster we can get you married."

Emily was relieved. She wasn't sure she could think of everything she needed to say without help, so she was thrilled to be able to do it with Harriett. Harriett handed her a piece of paper and a pen, so she quickly wrote, "Dear Benjamin, Abbie and Georgie, I enjoyed reading your letter. I have never served a meal of bacon sandwiches in my life, and I work as a cook for a living. Rest assured you will have a variety of food if you choose me to be your new mama." She looked up and read what she'd written aloud.

Harriett smiled and nodded. "That's good. Answer their direct questions and requirements first, and then you can go on and add the other pertinent details. You finish that part, and let me know when you need help with the things you need to include."

Emily dipped her pen in the inkwell, then put the pen to paper and wrote, "I love reading to children, especially girls, at any time of day, and I'm sure that will translate well to daughters, although I've never had one and can't be absolutely certain about that. I'm an adequate seamstress and know exactly how a little girl's hair should look, so there are no problems there. I expect children to make a mess, because if they couldn't make messes, they couldn't learn. I love to bake, and enjoy both picnicking and walks in the woods, although I've not had a lot of time for either in my busy life. I'm very sorry to hear about the loss of your wife. I lost my father at a very young age and know from personal experience how hard it is to grow up with only one parent. I'm more than willing to help out in a mercantile and would enjoy it immensely. I am twenty years old, and my name is Emily Hughes. I live with my mother in Beckham, Massachusetts. I've never been to Minnesota, or anywhere outside of Massachusetts, but would like to go there." When she was finished writing, Emily read the letter she'd written to Harriett. "What else should I add?"

"You want to tell them what you look like, and what interests you. Ask if they have any pets or anything else you want to know about them."

Emily nodded and wrote quickly, "I am a short woman with auburn hair and blue eyes. I enjoy reading when I have time and taking walks to enjoy nature. What do you like to do as a family? What are the girls interested in? Are there any other questions you have for me?" Again, she read what she'd written aloud.

Harriett smiled. "I think that's perfect. Sign it and I'll send it off with the mail tomorrow. We'll expect a response in a month or so." She squeezed Emily's hand. "If we don't have you married off before your mother needs you out of the house, you can stay here for a few days, but I do believe we'll have you on a train for Minnesota within the next two months."

Emily stood. "Thank you for the cookies and tea and for your time. I appreciate you helping me."

Harriett stood as well. As Emily watched her slowly gain her feet, she wondered again about the limp. It would be impolite to ask, though, so she brushed it off and headed for the door. Harriett saw her out. "Come see me in three and a half weeks and we'll talk about where to go from there."

Emily left the house and headed for home, her heart filled with trepidation. She needed to focus on the idea of being a mother to two little girls who needed her and helping her mother by leaving. She needed to do her best not to think about the fact she'd be marrying a man she'd never met. She couldn't think about that. The family did seem like a good one, and she only hoped she could find the courage to go through with the plans she'd set into motion.

CHAPTER 2

*B*enjamin smiled as he gave Mrs. Anderson her change. "Thanks for coming in Mrs. Anderson."

"Where else would I go? You're the only mercantile in town!" Mrs. Anderson was a straight-shooting woman in her mid-seventies. Benjamin was always glad to see her, because it meant her arthritis wasn't acting up too much for her to walk to the store. Sometimes, she would send a messenger over with her list and Benjamin would deliver it when he got off work for the day.

"You could always drive to St. Paul."

She shook her head. "My bones are too old for that, Benjamin. I'll walk right over here to your mercantile any day of the week."

"You look just as spry as ever, Mrs. Anderson. If I didn't know how much you loved Mr. Anderson, I'd ask if I could come calling." He gave her a slow wink to punctuate his words. He'd learned early on that flirting with his elderly customers helped them to come back, and he genuinely liked Mrs. Anderson. She never gossiped and was always pleasant to be around.

She chuckled. "You're a naughty boy, Benjamin." She leaned heavily on her cane as she walked toward the door, her shopping basket tucked over her arm.

The bell on the door tinkled, and they both turned to see who was coming into the store. "*Mor*, are you coming to keep my daughters and me from starving to death?"

Mrs. Anderson smiled and nodded at Ingrid Johnson. "You need to watch this silver-tongued boy of yours, Ingrid. He's been flirting with me, and here I am, old enough to be his grandmother." She walked slowly out the door and waved over her shoulder to Benjamin as she left the store.

Ingrid smiled at her son. "I brought some bread and a big pot of stew for you and the girls for supper. It's enough for two nights, so make it stretch." She held up a letter. "Who is this Harriett Long who is writing to you from Massachusetts? What are you hiding from me?" She said the words as if they were a joke, but he could tell by the narrowing of her eyes, she was serious.

Benjamin sighed. He'd hoped to put off this discussion for longer, but what could he do? "I've sent off for a mail order bride. The girls need a woman around the house, and I don't have it in me to try and court someone right now."

"But what about Kristen? I talked to her about you, and she's willing to have you call on her." Kristen was a local Norwegian girl who lived a few miles out of town. Benjamin had known her all his life, and simply wasn't interested in her. She was nice enough, but he wasn't attracted to her.

"I'm sorry, *Mor*. I don't think she's what I'm looking for." He held his hand out for the letter. How could he explain to his mother that Kristen was too much like Anna? He didn't want to be married to someone who would remind him of his dead wife for the rest of his life.

"So you're willing to just gamble someone who you don't even know will be a good mother to my grandbabies?"

17

"It's my life, and it's my decision. I'm their father. May I please have my letter?" His empty hand was still hanging in the air waiting.

She slapped it into his hand. "Don't you come crying to me when she turns out to be an awful woman who doesn't even know how to cook a simple Norwegian dish. Why you'd send for a mail order bride is simply beyond me. Kristen is just perfect and she's only a few miles away." She mumbled something to herself as she headed for the door. He was thankful he couldn't hear what it was. "I'll put your stew and bread in your house and spend a little time with my girls." The door slammed behind her, leaving him in no doubt about how she felt about the letter in his hand.

He slipped the letter into his pocket without reading it. He wanted to read it with the girls so they could all make the decision together. Their opinion on the matter was just as important as his. If he read it before he arrived home, he could make up his mind and be disappointed if they didn't agree with him. No, it would affect them all, and they'd decide as a family.

After closing up shop for the day, Benjamin slipped out the back to the house he shared with the girls. He could smell the pot of stew cooking and inhaled deeply. His *mor* wasn't perfect, but she was a wonderful cook, and he was fortunate to have her. "Girls! I'm home!"

The girls came running to see him each hugging him tightly. "*Farmor* came and brought supper. We don't have to have bacon sandwiches tonight!" Georgie was bouncing up and down.

Benjamin smiled. "Maybe we'll be done with bacon sandwiches soon." He pulled the letter out of his pocket. "Look what came in the mail today."

"Is it from our mail order mama?" Abbie asked.

Benjamin nodded. "At least it's from someone who wants

to be our mail order mama. We'll read it after supper and see if she'll suit us. Who's hungry?"

The girls quickly set the table while Benjamin served them each a bowl of stew and cut up the bread.

Once he'd done the supper dishes, they all sat at the table together to listen to Benjamin read the letter. The girls interrupted repeatedly as they liked what was said. "She's a cook, Papa. No more bacon!" Georgie couldn't get past the idea of having a mother who would cook for them.

"She likes to read *and* go for walks. Oh, Papa. Let's marry *her*!" Abbie insisted.

Once he was done, he set the letter down, his mind racing. If he sent her train tickets with this letter, she could be there in as little as three weeks. Two weeks for the letter to get to Beckham, a few days to prepare, and a five day train ride. He'd have to close the shop for a day to drive into St. Paul, but it would be worth the lost income. It was Friday, and they could drive into St. Paul Sunday when the store was closed anyway to buy the tickets for her to come out. He'd buy tickets for her to leave Massachusetts two weeks from Wednesday and they could pick her up on the following Monday. In twenty four days he could have a mother for his girls.

"We'll skip church on Sunday and drive to St. Paul to buy her a train ticket. Would you girls like that?"

Georgie jumped up and down clapping her hands while Abbie smiled and nodded happily.

Benjamin had Abbie bring him a pen, paper and ink so he could write a letter to send with the ticket. He was glad it was so easy to pick out a new mama for his girls.

～

IT HAD BEEN three and a half weeks since she'd mailed the

letter, so Emily decided to stop off at Harriett's house on her way home from work. It had been a hectic Thursday at work, because the Walters were having another dinner party. The parties were happening more and more often, multiplying her work load. Today, Mrs. Walters had asked her to dust the entire downstairs of the house as well so it would look good for her guests. Emily had barely finished fixing the meal when it was time for the guests to arrive.

She inhaled the scent of the autumn air as she walked. She loved the fall when the leaves were changing colors and the air was cool, but not cold. She enjoyed the sound of the leaves crackling under her feet as she headed down Rock Creek Road. She slowed her steps as she neared her destination, afraid there had been a letter and the family didn't want her, but more afraid there had been a letter and the family *did* want her. She all but dragged her feet as she headed to the front door, and taking a deep breath, she knocked.

Higgins answered again. "It's good to see you again, Miss Hughes." He opened the door wide to let her in. "Please follow me." He led her down the hall to the parlor Harriett used as an office. "Miss Hughes is here to see you, Ma'am."

Harriett rose to her feet. "Thank you, Higgins."

"Tea and cookies, Ma'am?"

"Yes, please." Harriett waited until he'd closed the door behind him before addressing Emily. "Your letter arrived yesterday. I haven't read it, because you should be the one to do that. Please sit down." She turned and headed to her desk.

Emily sank onto the rose patterned sofa and waited while Harriett dug through the papers on her desk. Once she'd produced the letter and handed it to Emily, Harriett sat down in her chair and turned her attention to other work while Emily read her letter.

"Dear Emily, You sound like exactly what our family needs. I've enclosed tickets for a train from Beckham,

Massachusetts to St. Paul, Minnesota. You'll need to switch trains in Chicago. I will close my shop for the day and meet you at the station in St. Paul. Live Oak is a two hour drive north of St. Paul, so after you arrive we'll return here to marry. My girls are very excited to know you will be arriving soon. I'll see you on the fifteenth of October at the train station. I will not have the girls with me. I'm a tall blond Norwegian man and will have a sign with your name on it. I look forward to meeting you. Best, Benjamin."

Emily took a deep breath to try to calm herself. This was what she wanted and needed, so why was she so frightened? "He's sent me train tickets for Wednesday of next week."

Harriett smiled happily. "That's wonderful. It's just what you need." She took the letter from Emily and skimmed over it, taking the check that had been sent for her services and placing it aside. There was also a small sum of money for Emily's needs which she handed to the younger woman along with the train tickets. "Let's go over what you'll need to take with you."

Harriett had a list of things she gave to each of the young brides she sent off. She handed it to Emily to skim over. "I don't have a wedding dress," Emily muttered.

"Well, there's enough money there to get one. It doesn't have to be a traditional wedding dress, though it would be nice. We'll see what we can find."

Emily read a few more things on the list and handed it back. "I wish I had time to make a new wardrobe, because my clothes are hopelessly out of fashion, but I don't. I hope my new family won't mind." She hated the idea of going to her new family with her old clothes, but she had no time to make more. She barely had time to get used to the idea before she was leaving. Was this really a good idea?

Harriett smiled, squeezing the younger woman's hand. "I don't think that will be a problem. Your future husband owns a mercantile so you'll be able to get what you need relatively quickly."

"I'm really nervous. I'm not sure this is what I should be doing," Emily confessed.

"I understand. You have every reason to be nervous, but this is an answer to your prayers. Your situation is a tough one, and we couldn't have found a better family for you." Harriett's voice was soothing and calm. "Would it help you if I went to the train station with you to see you off?"

Emily nodded slowly. "Would you mind?" She knew it was a lot to ask of a virtual stranger, but Harriett had been so sweet to offer, and she really didn't want to go alone.

"Not at all! I'm sending you off into an unknown situation. What time does your train leave on Wednesday?"

Emily glanced at the ticket to check. "Ten in the morning."

"Why don't you come to my house around half past eight? We'll walk to the station together."

Emily stood. "Thank you for all your help."

Harriett gripped Emily's hands between her own. "It's not a problem. If you need anything between now and when you leave Beckham, I want you to let me know right away."

"I will."

Harriett walked her to the door, and Emily waved goodbye. She took the long way home as she walked through the dark streets of Beckham. She'd never been further than five miles from the town, and she couldn't imagine what it would be like to leave and never see it again.

When she arrived home, she found her mother waiting for her in the parlor. "I was getting worried. You were out so late!" Emily had always come straight home after work, and although she'd known she'd be going to see Harriett that evening, she hadn't wanted to involve her mother and have her worried about Emily's decision before it was officially made.

Emily joined Jane on the sofa. "I'm sorry I worried you. I was speaking with Harriett Long. Do you know her?"

Jane seemed to think about it for a moment. She knew the name, but wasn't sure if she'd ever met the woman. "I'm not sure. Why?"

"Well, she's matching women who need husbands up with men in the west. I'm going to be a mail order bride." Emily spoke quickly to get the words out. She hadn't been looking forward to telling her mother what her decision had been.

Jane's eyes widened with surprise. "Where will you go?"

"I've agreed to marry a man in Minnesota. He lost his wife a few months ago, and he needs a mother for his two young daughters. They seem like a very nice family." She held up the letter and train tickets for her mother to see.

"When will you leave?"

"Wednesday morning. I'll be married on October fifteenth in the small town in Minnesota where he lives." Emily's eyes met her mother's, quietly pleading with her to find a way for her to stay. Surely William would change his mind rather than send her off to live with total strangers halfway across the continent.

Jane squeezed Emily's hand. "I'm so happy you found a good situation. I'll miss you, of course, but we can always write." Jane looked extremely relieved to know Emily had found a good place to go.

"I'll miss you, too." Emily tried not to let her mother see how upset she was by the idea of going off to Minnesota. "I need to figure out what to wear for my wedding," she said changing the subject abruptly. "I don't think I have anything suitable at all." She knew her mother would help her solve her little problem and they could quit talking about her move. She didn't want to cry in front of her mother at the prospect of going away, and focusing on the task at hand would be the perfect way to distract them both.

"Why don't you wear the dress I wore to marry your father?"

"You still have it?" Emily asked in surprise. They'd been sewing frantically trying to get a dress ready for her mother to wear when she married William. "Why aren't you wearing it for your own wedding?"

Jane smiled. "It's much too small for me now, but it should fit you perfectly. Besides, I couldn't marry another man in the dress I wore to marry your father. It wouldn't be right." She stood up, excitement dancing in her eyes. She was still slender, but when she'd married she'd been reed thin like her daughter. "Let's go see if it fits!" She hurried through their small house and up the stairs to her bedroom. She knelt in front of the chest at the foot of her bed and opened it. Emily had always thought of the chest as her mother's treasure box.

Emily stood watching as her mother dug through the box. She took several things out and stroked them. "This was your first church dress. You only wore it a few times, but you were so pretty in it." She dug some more. "This is the quilt I made you when I was carrying you." She laid it on top of the small dress. "Ahh, here it is." Jane pulled out a long white dress covered in lace. She held it up in front of her. "What do you think?"

Emily reached out and touched the lace on the dress. It was old-fashioned, but beautiful and so many women wore their mother's dresses to marry, it being old fashioned wouldn't matter a bit. "I love it. Do you think it'll fit?"

"I think so. We'll probably have to take it in a bit in the waist, and we'll definitely have to shorten it, but I think it'll work out very well for you. Let me help you try it on, and we can make the adjustments before you go."

Emily hugged her mother tightly. "Thank you for letting me wear your beautiful dress." The dress made her excited for the wedding for the first time. She had never worn anything so beautiful.

Jane smiled. "I'm happy that you want to. I only wish I could be there to see you married in it."

Emily nodded sadly. "I know. I won't be there for your wedding either." She wished she could see her mother's happiness on her wedding day, but knew it was impossible.

"I'm not sure what I'm going to do without you."

"You're going to be happy with your new husband. That's what you're going to do!"

~

EMILY WAS THRILLED to be able to give her notice at work the following morning. She didn't feel at all badly for what Mrs. Walters referred to as her abandonment. "You've been with us for three years! How can you just leave this way?"

"I can't come to work here when I'm living in Minnesota. I'm sure you'll find someone else to cook for you." And clean and watch your children for you. "My last day will be Tuesday."

"But it's Friday! I can't possibly find someone else so soon."

Emily found the idea didn't bother her a bit. She didn't mind leaving Mrs. Walters in a bind after the way she'd treated her. "You may have to do for yourself for a few days, but it won't be the end of the world."

Mrs. Walters frowned. "Are you getting snide with me?"

"No, Ma'am. I would never do that." *I'd love to, but I need the last few days of work*, she thought.

After Mrs. Walters left her alone in the kitchen to work, Emily had to refrain from shouting for joy. She was nervous about the wedding, but she was thrilled to leave her job behind.

∾

EVERY EVENING EMILY and her mother worked together on their wedding dresses. Emily was glad she'd have this last memory of her mother to take with her. They talked and laughed about different things they'd done together over the years. Emily talked to her mother about the first letter she'd received from the Johnson family where the girls had requested someone who knew how to cook more than bacon and wouldn't ever fix bacon sandwiches for dinner.

Jane laughed aloud. "That man is lost without a wife beside him. The poor girls. I bet they're ready to have you there."

"It certainly does sound like it. I can't wait to meet them. He's going to be meeting me in St. Paul at the train station, but he won't be bringing the girls." She wished he would, because it would be easier for her, but there was no time to write him to request that, and she doubted she would make the request even if there had been time.

"At least you won't have to worry about them being upset that he's remarrying. It sounds like they practically begged him to place the ad."

"That's the impression I got from the letters." Emily held her dress in front of her. "I think I'm finished." She looked down at it to be certain she hadn't made any mistakes. A mistake on a regular dress was bad enough. A mistake on her wedding dress would be terrible, because it would be the first impression most people would have of her. She hoped he hadn't invited more than a handful of people to the wedding.

"Go try it on! I want to see how it looks." It was late

Tuesday evening. They both should have been in bed hours before, but the dress needed to be finished. Emily knew she could always sleep on the train.

She had grown more and more nervous by the day. Her first train ride and a wedding all in one week. It was enough to give a woman heart palpitations.

She ran up the narrow stairs to her bedroom to change. Once she was in her room, she looked around her. All of her personal belongings were gone. The only things left were the sturdy bed she'd slept on since she was a small girl, a small dresser and an armoire against one wall. All of her clothes were neatly pressed and in a carpet bag. It saddened her to realize everything she owned fit into such a small bag.

She stripped out of her dress and pulled the wedding dress over her head. It was tight in the waist, but fell comfortably around her hips and stopped just above her shoes. She walked down the stairs where her mother waited.

When Emily walked into the parlor where she'd been sewing with Jane, her mother covered her mouth with one hand, tears springing to her eyes. "Oh, Emily. You look so beautiful."

Emily smiled. She knew she wasn't really beautiful, and it was just a mother's love that made it seem so, but still it felt good to hear the words. She turned in a slow circle. "Is the hem straight?"

"It's perfect. It's absolutely perfect. If your father could see you now, he would be so proud of the young lady you've become." Jane set her dress to the side and walked to her daughter, pulling her into a tight embrace. "I'm going to miss you so much."

Emily hugged her back. "I'll miss you too, Mama." She pulled back. "Just think, in a week, I'm going to be married with two daughters of my own." The idea was still baffling to her, but she acted as if it were an everyday occurrence to travel across the country to marry a complete stranger.

Jane swiped at a tear running down her cheek. "It's so hard to believe my daughter is old enough to marry. Promise me you'll write often."

Emily sniffed back a tear of her own. "Of course, I will. I promise."

~

HARRIETT HERSELF ANSWERED the door when Emily knocked the following morning. "Are you all ready?" Harriett looked the younger woman up and down taking her measure.

Emily nodded. "I finished my wedding dress just last night. I didn't have time to make any other clothes, but you're right, I can handle that when I get to Minnesota."

Harriett stepped onto the front porch, and they walked together toward the train station. "Do you have your ticket and the spending money Mr. Johnson sent you? You'll need the money for food on the train." She patted the small bag over her shoulder. "I packed you some sandwiches that will work for today to get you started."

"Oh, thank you!" Emily was surprised by the other woman's small act of kindness. "Yes, I have everything. I even have the dress I wore to church my first day there and the quilt my mother made for me before I was born."

Harriett eyed the bag Emily carried. "I hope you remembered to pack some clothes as well." She sounded doubtful as she looked at the size of the bag.

Emily laughed. "I only have two work dresses, a Sunday dress, and now my wedding dress. There was plenty of room for other things." Emily was wearing her Sunday dress and a long winter coat. It was getting chilly in the mornings now that they were well into October. "Thank you for seeing me off. It does make it easier for me."

When they arrived at the train station the two women sat together and spoke loudly to be heard over the din. "I want you to write to me as soon as you get to Minnesota. After you've been married a week or two, you need to write again so I'll know you're in a good situation. If anything is wrong, we'll find a way to get you out."

"What do you mean?" Emily asked. Marriage was forever. No matter what kind of situation she found herself in, she had no right to leave or even think about leaving. Surely Harriett knew that.

"Some men hit their wives or treat them badly. If that happens to you, even once, you need to write to me and I'll send you a train ticket home. Do you understand?" The look in Harriett's eyes was intense as she spoke.

Emily nodded, wondering why Harriett was bringing it up. "I will." She didn't think she could, but it seemed so important to Harriett, she would agree to anything to give the other woman peace of mind.

"There's no reason for any woman to ever stay in a bad situation. All women should be told that before they marry."

"I'll remember."

The conductor called then. "All aboard!"

Emily stood. "I guess this is goodbye. Thank you for all your help, and I'll write as soon as I get there." It seemed strange that she felt such a close friendship with this woman when they'd only met a few times. She was truly going to miss her, though.

"I appreciate it. I'll be watching for your letter."

On impulse Emily hugged the other woman goodbye. "Thanks for being my friend when I needed one."

Harriett clutched the younger woman to her. "Everyone deserves to have a friend when they need one."

Harriett stood watching the younger woman until she was on the train, and then watched as the train pulled out of the station. She said a quick prayer the girl would find what she needed in Minnesota before turning to walk home through the streets of Beckham. She wouldn't receive the letter telling her Emily was safe fast enough.

CHAPTER 3

*E*mily felt overwhelmed by the huge crowd at the St. Paul train station. How was she going to be able to spot Benjamin with all these people around? She fought the panic rising in her throat and concentrated on what he'd told her in his letter. He was a tall blond and would be holding a sign with her name on it. She was short enough she had to stand on tiptoe to see over the shoulders of the people in front of her. Had he decided not to come? What would she do if he left her stranded there at the train station?

She hated crowds and the panic that came from being in the center of one was getting worse and worse. She needed to find him and get out of the city as quickly as she could, but the longer she stood there, the harder it became for her to see out through the crowd. She forced herself to breathe slowly and evenly. *Please, God, let this crowd move so I can see him.*

The couple in front of her moved off and she could finally see out over the ocean of faces. Off to the side, she saw a tall man holding a sign painted on a piece of wood over his head. It read, "Emily Hughes." She breathed a sigh of relief, picked up her bag and made her way to the man weaving in and out of people on her way. She stopped in front of him and mumbled, "I'm Emily."

He looked at her in surprise for a moment. She'd said she was short, but this girl couldn't be twenty, could she? She was much too small to be the one he was looking for. "You're Emily Hughes? Here to marry Benjamin Johnson?" he asked in a big booming voice.

She nodded. Why did he look so surprised? She'd described herself. Was she not what he'd expected?

Why does she look like she's afraid of her own shadow? he wondered.

He took her bag from her hand and led her to his buggy. In his mind, she'd been taller and blonder. Sure, she'd told him she was a brunette, but somehow, in his mind, she looked just like Anna. She wasn't what he'd expected in a bride, and he found himself instantly disappointed. Anna had been so outgoing, everyone crowded around her everywhere she went. He imagined Emily would be the one hiding in the corner at church socials so she didn't actually have to talk to anyone.

And her clothes. What was she thinking coming out here to get married in clothes that were so ragged? Did she not realize he was a businessman and he needed his wife to live up to his reputation? He hoped she'd packed something suitable to be married in.

When they reached his buggy, he put his bag in the back and held out his hand to help her into her seat. She'd rarely ridden behind a horse. She and her mother had never owned one. They'd been able to walk everywhere they needed to go in their small town.

Once she was seated, he walked around and climbed up beside her. "Did you have a good journey?"

"It was nice, thank you."

She spoke so softly, he could barely hear her. "The girls are very excited to meet you. They've talked about nothing but getting a new mama for weeks."

"I'm glad." She didn't look at him choosing to stare down at her hands instead.

"I thought about bringing them with me, but it's a long drive, so I left them with my parents last night."

"I'm excited to meet them." She really wished he would have brought them. She would have felt a great deal more comfortable with the children there. She had no idea what to say to a man. She wasn't sure she'd ever been alone with a man before, so she felt out of her element. She'd been so quiet and shy during her school years she'd never even had a beau. It was easier for her that way.

"So you were a cook back East?" He navigated the busy streets skillfully happy to see they were almost out of town. He should be able to hear her better once they didn't have the noise from the city around them.

"Yes."

"Were you a cook in a restaurant?" How many questions could he ask before he ran out of things to say? Surely, she'd respond to something with more than one sentence.

"No, for a family in town."

"What type of food can you cook?"

She shrugged. "I never really thought about it. Just normal food, I guess."

Finally, they were away from the noise of the city. "Normal food? Do you cook any Norwegian foods?" He knew his mother would be much happier if she could at least cook Norwegian dishes.

"I couldn't even tell you what dishes are Norwegian. What are some Norwegian foods?"

He glanced at her in surprise. "Rakfisk, lutefisk, syltelabb, smalahove, pickled herring?" At her blank stare, he chuckled. "Well, maybe *Mor* can teach you to cook Norwegian."

"*Mor*?"

"It's the Norwegian word for mother. What nationality are you?" Maybe he could get her talking about her heritage. He didn't want to make the long drive back home with her sitting in total silence. Talking to Anna had never been an effort. Maybe *Mor* was right and he was making a big mistake.

She shrugged. "Irish, French and English, I believe."

"So your family has been here for a long time I take it?" So much for that potential conversation. What could he possibly persuade her to talk about? Was she this shy with everyone, or was it simply because she knew they'd be married in a few hours?

"Yes. Yours?"

"My parents immigrated here from Norway."

"They live near you?" She knew he was trying to get her to talk with him, but she was having a hard time knowing what to say. She was always shy, but this was the worst it had ever been. Her mother had explained about the wedding night to her, and knowing she'd be doing *that* with him in just a few hours was nerve wracking.

He nodded. "All of my family is in Minnesota. Most are close." He liked having family nearby.

"Do you have a big family?"

"I have seven brothers and four sisters."

Her eyes widened. "And they're all close enough that I'll meet them soon?" She tried to keep the dread from her voice. She hoped they wouldn't all be there for the wedding. She didn't think she could handle meeting that many new people all on one day. It was hard enough just meeting him and the girls.

"Yes, you'll meet most of them this evening at the wedding supper."

"Wedding supper? You had time to plan a wedding supper?" Why had she pictured him and the girls with her for the wedding and them all standing in front of the preacher together? She hadn't seen this as a normal wedding with a big group of people. How was she going to handle being the center of attention that way? She felt the panic rising in her throat again, but tried to hide how very afraid she was of the idea.

"It's just going to be at my parents' house. Nothing formal and just family." Why was she nervous about meeting his family? Surely she'd realized he and his girls wouldn't be isolated with no family around.

"That's a lot of people, though. Sounds like your family is the entire state of Minnesota!"

He laughed. "Not even close. There are a lot of us, though. I'm the youngest, so you'll meet lots of brothers and sisters and nephews and nieces today." Now that she was actually talking to him, she didn't seem to be so bad. "How many brothers and sisters do you have?"

"I'm an only child. My father died when I was two, and my mother never remarried. She's getting married next month, though." She stared out at the scenery as they drove through the countryside. She was surprised by how pretty Minnesota was. The carriage was small enough they were pressed together from shoulder to hip. She wished she could move a respectable distance away, but they'd be married in a few hours so it probably didn't matter too much except in her mind.

He hadn't been sure how he'd react physically to his bride, but he found he liked the way she was pressed against him. At first, he hadn't liked her appearance, simply because it was so different from Anna's, but the more time he spent with her, the more he realized that he was looking forward to his wedding night. "Is that why you answered my letter?"

She nodded. "My mother's fiancé didn't like the idea of having me there after the wedding. It was either become a mail order bride or find a family who would hire me as a live in servant. My experience with the family I've been working for made me decide I'd rather be a mail order bride."

"What happened with them?"

She thought for a moment about the best way to answer him. "I've been working for the same family for the past three years. I was hired to be a cook, but it's gradually become more and more. For the past few months, I've been expected to cook not only three meals per day, but also do all the dusting and cleaning and take care of the two children. None of that would bother me if my pay had risen with my duties. If they'd paid me for everything I'd done, I'd have been able to find a place to live and support myself." She sighed. "I was looking for a different position in the local paper when my mother told me about her marriage."

He thought about what she'd told him. "You were right to get out of that situation. I'm glad you came out here to be part of our family." He took her hand, which was resting on her lap, and squeezed it in his own.

She felt her hand tingling where he held it. She looked down and saw how huge his hand was compared to hers and felt overwhelmed again. He dwarfed her in every way. "Tell me about the bacon sandwiches." She wondered how it would be to kiss a man who was so much bigger than her. Or any man for that matter. Was it wrong to think about kissing him? They would be married in a few hours, so maybe it was okay.

He laughed. "Bacon is about the only thing I can cook. *Mor* brings bread into town for us every other day or so, and will usually bring a meal with her. If she doesn't bring enough food to last until her next visit, the girls are stuck with eating bread and jam or bacon sandwiches. I'd just made bacon sandwiches again right before my girls and I sat down to write that letter."

It was just as she'd guessed. "So your girls would give just about anything to never have to eat another bacon sandwich?" If they were that sick of bacon, they would love her on sight. Even in her modesty, she knew she was an excellent cook. The comments she received from the dinner parties she'd cooked for had left her in no doubt about that.

He shrugged. "The younger one especially. She's got more spirit in her. The older one thanks me sweetly every time I put anything on the table." And that worried him. He knew Abbie was as sick of bacon sandwiches as he and Georgie were, but she seemed almost afraid to say anything about it. Emily actually reminded him a bit of Abbie.

"They sound like lovely children. I can't wait to meet them." Even though she was nervous about being a wife and about meeting his family, she was excited at the prospect of having two little girls to love.

"They've been calling you their 'Mail Order Mama' ever since you answered the letter. I hope they'll shorten it to just 'Mama' after we marry, but I'm not certain they will." He felt the need to warn her there could be some slips from the girls.

"I won't mind either way. They can even call me Emily until they feel more comfortable with something else."

He shook his head. "No, that wouldn't be respectful."

They drove along in silence for a few minutes, and she realized he was still holding her hand. She found she didn't mind at all. It felt good to be touched.

By the time they reached his town, she was happy to see the buildings rising before them. She had never been much of a conversationalist, and had found it difficult to keep up her end of the conversation with the handsome stranger sitting beside her.

He pointed out his mercantile with the huge sign reading "Benjamin's Bargains".

"Do you get a lot of business?" she asked.

"I'm the only mercantile in town and all the surrounding farmers shop at my store. I do a good business." He looked over at her. "I'll be asking for your help from time to time. Maybe a couple of hours in the afternoon, or taking a whole day here and there. The girls are good at staying out of trouble while I work."

He pulled up in front of a small house just down from the church. "I thought we were on our way to get married."

He nodded and walked around the buggy, helping her down. "We are. My sister said to bring you to her house first. She insisted you'd need to take a bath after so many days on the train and you might need help with your hair." He pulled his pocket watch out and looked at it. "We have just over an hour before the wedding."

He reached into the back and pulled her bag out, carrying it for her up to the small house. He knocked on the door and a tall blond woman opened it. "Birgitta, this is my bride, Emily. Emily, my sister, Birgitta."

Emily smiled glad to meet one of his siblings before the others, so she wouldn't be as overwhelmed later. "It's nice to meet you." She knew her voice had dropped to a mere whisper again.

Birgitta's eyes met Benjamin's over Emily's head. "She's tiny!" She opened her door wide. "Come in. Come in! We must get you ready for your wedding." She pointed her finger at Benjamin. "You go away. We'll see you at the church. Go make sure *Mor* has your pretty girls ready."

Benjamin squeezed Emily's arm. "Don't let my sister bully

you." He turned and walked toward his store his strides long and hurried.

Emily watched him go, and then turned to Birgitta. "I'm filthy. I can't believe how dirty the train was." She was embarrassed to meet anyone looking like she did, so she was thankful it was just one person. It was bad enough to meet Benjamin like this.

Birgitta wrapped her arm around Emily's shoulders. "I have a bath waiting for you in the kitchen. I just need to add hot water, and it's already boiling." She steered Emily toward the kitchen and added the hot water. "You can go ahead and take your clothes off. I have daughters and sisters, and you won't bother me. I'll wash your hair for you."

Emily had never taken off her clothes in front of anyone but her mother, but she was afraid to say 'no' to the older woman. She stripped quickly and sank into the warm water.

Dropping to her knees beside the tub, Birgitta used a glass and poured it over Emily's head and then scrubbed it with soap. After she finished washing Emily's hair, she scrubbed her back for her.

Emily sighed. No one had washed her back for her since she was a small child. "That feels nice. Thank you."

After a moment, Birgitta stood up. "I wish I could let you soak for an hour, but we need to get you ready for your wedding." She walked over to the work table and got a towel she'd placed there earlier. She held it out and turned her head, so she could wrap it around Emily without making her uncomfortable.

"You dry off, and I'll be right back. I want to get a couple of things for you."

While she was gone, Emily dressed hurriedly in her chemise. She pulled her dress which had been carefully wrapped in tissue paper out of her bag and spread it out on the table. It didn't look terribly wrinkled so she pulled it over her head. She buttoned it up the back, just finishing up as Birgitta came back into the room.

Birgitta held a small bouquet of white and pink flowers. She had two single white flowers in her hand. "I thought you might like to carry this bouquet, and we can put these two in your hair."

Emily smiled utterly charmed by the details Birgitta was thinking of. "Oh, thank you. I'd love to wear them." She took one of the single flowers and held it under her nose to smell it. "What kind of flower is this?"

"They're asters. There aren't a lot of flowers still in bloom this time of year in Minnesota."

"They're perfect. Thank you for thinking of them." Emily was glad she'd have a piece of Benjamin's home with her as she walked down the aisle toward him.

"Your dress is lovely. If you sit, I'll fix your hair for you."

Emily sat down on one of the straight back wooden chairs in the kitchen. Each one had a cushion made in a red check pattern that matched the pretty table cloth. Looking around the kitchen for the first time, Emily found it lovely. The curtains matched the tablecloth and there were small paintings on the walls. "I like the way you've decorated your kitchen."

"Thank you!" She used Emily's brush and comb to quickly comb through her hair and deftly applied pins to put it into an updo. She added a flower to one side and tilted her head to the side to look at her. "I think you'll look better with just the one flower in your hair. Is that okay with you?"

Emily nodded. "That's fine."

Birgitta took a small hand mirror from the table where she'd laid it and held it up for Emily. "What do you think?"

Emily stared at her reflection in the mirror for a moment. "I love it." She really did like how it looked, but she knew she'd have lied and said she liked it even if she hadn't. She'd do anything to keep from offending this sweet woman who had gone so far out of her way to make her happy and comfortable.

"You look beautiful. My brother will swallow his tongue when he sees you walking through the church toward him."

Emily knew better. Benjamin was looking for a mother for his daughters nothing more. She looked at the clock on the wall. "We only have ten minutes. Shouldn't we go?"

"Yes, we need to leave. It's a short walk to the church, but it wouldn't do to be late for your own wedding." She went into the parlor and called out, "Dalla, Adam, Edna, Jarl, it's time to go!" Four tall blond teens, two boys and two girls ran into the room all dressed in their Sunday best clothes. "These are my children. The girls are Dalla and Edna, and the boys are Jarl and Adam." She opened the door and the children walked ahead to the church.

"Isn't your husband going to the wedding?"

"Lars is the pastor. He's already there."

"Oh! I didn't realize you were the pastor's wife." How could she live up to being in the same family as a pastor? Wouldn't people be watching her more closely?

"Yes, that's my lot in life." She smiled as they walked slowly toward the church. "He was a simple farmer when I married him and had my babies. Ten years ago, he told me he needed to answer the Lord's call."

"How did you feel about it?"

"Overwhelmed at first, but I think I've found my place." They stepped into the back of the church. "Our church doubles as our schoolhouse." She looked at Emily and fixed a stray tendril of hair before hugging her. "I'm so glad to be getting a new sister. I'm going to go take my seat. Wait until you hear the music."

Emily felt very alone at the back of the church. She wished she didn't have to walk down the aisle alone, but she'd have had to do that if she'd married back home as well. There were no men who had been father figures to her. She took deep steady breaths trying to calm her nerves. She hated being the center of attention!

After a moment, she heard the music start, and slowly walked around the corner and started walking up the aisle toward Benjamin. She saw two little blond heads in the front row peering at her with huge smiles and assumed they were the girls. They were sitting with an older woman who stared straight ahead, not even turning around to see the bride.

She walked straight to the front and took her place next to Benjamin. He smiled down at her as Lars, the pastor, cleared his throat and began speaking. Emily let the familiar words wash over her. She'd not been to a great deal of weddings, but several of her school friends had married and she'd attended. Everything passed in a blur and she was asked to face Benjamin. Benjamin spoke his vows in a strong voice that carried throughout the church. When it was Emily's turn she mumbled the words. Benjamin pushed a ring onto her finger and leaned down to kiss her for the first time. Lars pronounced them man and wife and introduced them to the assembled crowd as Mr. and Mrs. Johnson.

Emily faced the audience, trying not to make eye contact with anyone. After a moment she was nearly knocked over by the two blond girls she'd noticed on her way up the aisle. She squatted down in her dress to meet them for the first time.

"I'm Emily," she told them in her soft voice.

"You're our mail order mama!" The girl who spoke was the younger, so she immediately assumed she was Georgie.

"You must be Georgie," Emily told her smiling at the young girl.

Georgie nodded and pointed to her sister. "That's Abbie. We're really glad you're here."

"I'm so happy to meet you both." They hugged her again, and she stood back up next to Benjamin, urging the girls to stand with them.

Benjamin smiled down at her. "Thank you for making them part of our wedding."

"They're our children. Of course, they're part of the wedding." She squeezed the hand of the older girl who was standing at her side. She had recognized the look of shyness on the girl's face and was pleased she'd be able to relate well to one of them.

The four of them walked to the back of the church together, several people stopping Benjamin to shake his hand along the way. He introduced her to each of the people, but she knew she'd never remember their names. They went out to the buggy and he helped her in and put the girls in the back seat. "We're going to *Mor's* for the wedding supper. The girls will spend the night with my parents tonight, and we'll pick them up in the morning before I open the store at ten."

Emily swallowed hard at the thought of their wedding night. She wasn't yet ready to think about it, though, so she sat silently on the drive out to his parents' farm. "How long will it take to get there?" she asked after a while.

"It's a thirty minute drive," he told her. "I almost wish I hadn't agreed to a wedding supper after being on the road all day, but I thought you'd want to celebrate our wedding." He looked over at her as she watched the scenery. "You'd rather have skipped it, wouldn't you?"

She nodded. "It's okay, though. I'm just not good at meeting large groups of people all at once."

"I'm sorry. I should have waited and asked you." He pulled the buggy in front of a large farmhouse. "Here we are. I lived here until I married Anna." He walked around and helped her down while the girls scrambled down on their own.

43

Abbie walked over and slipped her small hand into Emily's. "I'll help you meet everyone."

Emily smiled. "Thank you, Abbie." Emily was glad Abbie was so much quieter than the rest of her large Norwegian family. Emily and Abbie walked into the house hand in hand.

Abbie led her straight to the woman who had refused to look at her in the church. "*Farmor*, this is our new mama, Emily." Abbie stood looking between the two women as if she expected something bad to happen.

"It's nice to meet you, Mrs. Johnson. Is there anything I can help you with?" Emily was proud of how steady she kept her voice. Every time she met someone new it was an effort to keep her voice loud enough to be heard.

Her new mother-in-law rounded on Emily, a scowl on her face. "Not unless you know about Norwegian cooking. Do you?" Her voice sounded angry.

Emily swallowed hard, determined to get along with her new mother-in-law. "No, Ma'am, but I'd be happy to learn."

"Just stay out of the way." Ingrid turned back to her stove and the strong odors coming from it.

Emily looked to see if anyone other than Abbie had noticed the exchange, but no one appeared to be paying any attention. The house was filled with blond Norwegians, and Emily felt out of place with her brunette hair. She moved out of the way as she'd been asked and went to speak to Birgitta, Abbie still clinging to her hand.

Birgitta introduced her to several of her siblings, none of whom Emily would later remember. She'd need to meet them one at a time to remember names and faces. Today, she was simply overwhelmed by them all.

Everyone was polite with the single exception of her mother-in-law. She refused to let it bother her, though. The woman simply didn't know her, and once she did, she'd come around. She had to.

She sat next to Benjamin for the meal, and once Lars had said the prayer for all of them, they ate the huge meal. She was only able to eat a few bites, but managed to make it look like more by pushing the food around on her plate. She didn't want to hurt anyone's feelings by not eating the food they'd cooked, but she was so nervous, her throat felt like it was closing up.

When it came time to cut the wedding cake, she glanced up at Benjamin as they held the knife together. They sliced through the cake and cut small slices for each of them. Emily took her fork and carefully fed a bite of the cake to Benjamin as she'd seen done at a wedding back home. When Benjamin returned the favor, she forced herself to chew, but the cake tasted like sawdust to her.

Abbie was still staying within a few feet of Emily at all times, obviously afraid her new mama was going to run off somewhere.

It was hours before the party finally ended, but it all passed in a blur for Emily. She talked to the girls as much as she could while Benjamin laughed and joked with his brothers. Emily would look up from time to time and always find Benjamin's eyes on her. She would blush and look down paying attention to whomever was speaking to her.

Once the guests had thinned out, Benjamin led Emily and the girls outside. "It's time for us to go home. We'll be back to get you first thing in the morning," Benjamin promised the girls.

Abbie reached out to cling to Emily's hand. "Can't we come home with you?"

Benjamin shook his head, squatting down until he was eye level with his older daughter. "I'll take good care of your new mama. I promise."

"I don't want her to go away." The fear of losing her new mother was apparent in Abbie's voice.

Emily hugged the child to her. "I'm not going anywhere. I came all this way on a train to be your mama. How could I leave now before we've had a chance to do anything fun together? I haven't gotten to read to you or bake you a cake or cookies. We haven't even been on a picnic or a walk through the woods. We're going to do all those things just as soon as we can. Okay?"

Abbie stared up at Emily in the darkness. "You promise?"

Emily stroked her cheek. "I promise." Emily knew she had her work cut out for her as she helped this little girl get over her fear of losing her. How could she explain to her that even if she had somewhere else to go, she wouldn't leave her?

"Me too?" Georgie asked, obviously not concerned just wanting to be included.

"We can't do anything fun without you, Georgie!" Emily told the younger girl hugging her as well.

She looked back at Abbie. "Are you okay?" She really hated the idea of leaving the little girl, not only for her, though. She was afraid of the wedding night, and knew if the girls were there, she could make an excuse to sit by Abbie's bed during the night.

Abbie nodded. "Tomorrow we'll have all day together?"

"I need to write two letters tomorrow, but I have nothing else planned for the whole day, except making a supper that is *not* bacon sandwiches. Will you girls help me with that?"

Abbie giggled. "We've had bacon sandwiches a lot since Mama died." She covered her mouth with her hand. "I'm sorry."

Emily shook her head, understanding immediately. "You had a mama before me you loved very much. You can talk to me about her anytime you want to. I'll even help you take flowers to her grave if you want."

Abbie flung her arms around Emily. "I'm so glad we picked you to be our new mama."

Emily bowed her head low over Abbie's and kissed the top of her head. "So am I." And she was. Being their mama was something she had been looking forward to. Being Benjamin's wife was the scary part.

Benjamin cleared his throat. "It's time for us to go. We'll be here early tomorrow morning. Be good for your *Farmor*."

"We're always good!" Georgie told him as he helped Emily into the buggy for the drive home. "We'll see you tomorrow, Papa and Mail Order Mama!"

"It's just Mama," Abbie corrected in a loud whisper.

"Bye, Mama!" Georgie yelled.

"G'night, Mama and Papa," Abbie told them, waving as they drove away.

As soon as they were on the road, Benjamin took Emily's hand in his. "Thank you so much for making my daughters feel so important. It means everything to me." As the day had progressed, she'd become prettier and prettier to him. He was sure it was the way she'd acted toward his daughters.

"Our daughters are important. I hated leaving them there." For more reasons than one.

"I know, but you and I need at least one night alone together." He slipped his arm around her shoulders and pulled her closer to him on the buggy seat. "Did I tell you how beautiful you look in your wedding gown?"

She shook her head staring up at him in wonder.

"Well, you do. You're a beautiful bride. Abbie was right. I'm really glad we chose you to be our mail order mama."

Emily blushed but laughed softly. "Your girls are wonderful. I'm really looking forward to getting to know them better."

He looked down at her in the light of the full moon. "What about me? Are you looking forward to getting to know me better?"

She bit her lip afraid he was talking about having marital

relations with her that evening. "I'm nervous about getting to know you better," she finally said, honestly.

"There's nothing to be nervous about." He kept his voice soft and gentle, determined not to frighten off his shy bride. When he'd courted Anna, she'd been as eager for love making as he was. They'd spent hours kissing and hugging and holding hands. They'd stroked one another until they were both desperate to be together. By the time they finally married, she had fallen eagerly into his arms. Emily's shyness was something he hadn't bargained for, but he had always had strong needs, and he wasn't going to put off his wedding night, just because his bride had a strong case of the jitters.

CHAPTER 4

*A*fter pulling the buggy in front of his house, Benjamin jumped down to help Emily to the ground. He opened the door and led her up the stairs. The store was on the ground floor, and the back stairs behind the store led up to their house. The house was still a two story home, but it simply started with the second level. He showed her the kitchen, parlor and dining room first, and then led her up the stairs. "It was built this way so we could live on the same property the store resides on. I like to be close to the store, because I feel like it stays safer this way. The girls can be left alone in the house during the day, because really, I'm still here."

"It's nice." She looked around at the pretty decorations on the walls and knew she'd be in no hurry to change anything. Anna had done a beautiful job with this house.

He opened the door to a guest bedroom first. "This room is just an extra. We'd hoped to have enough children to fill the whole place, but it never happened." There was sadness in his voice as he said the words.

"I'm sorry. She never got pregnant after Georgie?"

"She was pregnant when she died. She got scarlet fever in her fifth month and just never recovered. The rest of us had it too, but it didn't affect us like it did her."

"I'm so sorry." Her hand reached for his and squeezed it. It was the first time she'd touched him voluntarily and it felt strange to her, but good.

"Thank you." He led her to the next room and opened the door. It was a little girl's room. There was a pretty quilt on the bed along with a rag doll. A painting of a flower graced the wall. "This is Abbie's room. If you ever forget which room belongs to which child, Abbie's room is always spotless with everything put away and her bed made perfectly. On the other hand..." He opened the door to Georgie's room and Emily couldn't help but let out a quick laugh.

"Georgie's not quite so neat is she?" Georgie's room had the same pretty quilt on it, but hers was rumpled terribly. Her rag doll, identical to her sisters, was standing on its head on the dresser. There was a nightgown on the floor, half under the bed. There was a painting of a stream in front of a forest on the wall, but it was askew making the unkempt look even more obvious.

"This is actually very neat for Georgie. She made a real effort to make it look nice for you." Benjamin's eyes were twinkling as he spoke, acknowledging his younger daughter's flaw with amusement.

Emily's eyes met Benjamin's and she grinned. "I guess neatness will be one of the first things I work on with her." It was nice to have a place to start. She wondered what she would find to be Abbie's biggest flaw.

"It's going to have to be." He led her to the next room and opened the door wide. "This is our room. I cleared out the top two drawers for you." He dropped her bag on the bed. "If you need more space, just let me know."

"Thank you. I'm sure that will be more than enough." She

smiled ruefully at her bag with all her belongings in it. There was so little she had, she could probably make do with half a drawer.

"You can pick out some fabric from the store tomorrow so you can make some more dresses." He guessed correctly what she was thinking as he eyed her small bag.

She smiled her thanks. "I appreciate it. I'm sorry I came so ill-prepared. If I'd had another week or two, I could have had some dresses finished before I came." She wondered if he thought less of her for having so little. She hoped not, but there was little she could do about it now if he did. She'd just have to work extra hard to get some dresses made up as quickly as possible.

"You'll have plenty of time now to work on them. The girls need to be taught to sew anyway."

She looked around the room and saw the furniture looked sturdy. There was a large bed that she tried not to stare at as well as a dresser and a good sized armoire. In the corner was a rocking chair. She walked over to it and ran her hand across the seat.

He followed her and sat down on the bed. With him sitting and her standing, she was only slightly taller than him. What had she been thinking marrying a man who was so much larger than she was? He could hurt her so easily!

He caught her hand and pulled her toward him and down onto his lap. He cupped the back of her head with his hand and brought her lips to his. His tongue automatically traced the seam of her lips, and she wasn't sure what he was trying to do. She kept her mouth tightly closed and her hands on his shoulders to steady herself.

"Open your mouth for me," he whispered against her lips.

"What?" There was shock in her tone, but he didn't respond, simply slid his tongue into her open mouth. He nipped her bottom lip with his teeth while his tongue explored hers.

She'd never been kissed before their wedding, and it had never occurred to her a man would want to put his tongue in her mouth as he kissed her. She stayed rigid against him for a moment before relaxing into his embrace, her hands moving around to his back and stroking the muscles through his suit jacket.

His hands went around her back and he unbuttoned her to the waist, his hands exploring her body through her chemise. After a moment, he pulled back, his breathing heavy. "I'm going to go out and take care of the horses while you get ready for bed." He put her on her feet and she swayed a little but grabbed the armoire to steady herself.

Why had his kiss made her so weak in the knees? She'd never felt anything like that before. Of course, she'd never been kissed before today either, so maybe kissing was supposed to leave her weak in the knees.

He stood and left the room, and she heard the front door close behind him. She was in a daze as she put her clothes away in the drawers and changed into her nightgown. She left her dirty dress in her carpet bag with plans to see if anything else needed to be washed.

By the time she heard the door open again, she'd worked herself into a frenzy worried about what was going to happen. Her mother had explained how a man consummated a marriage, but she'd pictured a normal sized man. She couldn't imagine lying down and letting Benjamin lie on top of her. He'd crush her with his bulk. He wasn't fat; he was merely tall and muscular, and she was convinced she was too small to ever mate with a man of his size. Surely if she mentioned that to him he'd understand.

She was lying in the bed with the covers tucked under her chin when he walked into the room, and by the tension in her body, he could see that his attempts to relax her by kissing her before he left to put the horses up hadn't worked. She was more nervous than ever.

He sighed and turned off the lamp, wishing she would let him look at her, but he knew it was out of the question. It would make her even more nervous. He quickly undressed, happy that his body was hidden from her, not because he was embarrassed, but because he was fully aroused, and he was certain if she saw him now, she would be in a full blown panic.

He slipped between the sheets and lay on his side facing her, his chin propped up by one of his hands. His other hand stroked her cheek until she turned her face toward him. "There's nothing to worry about. I need you to trust me." His voice was low and gravelly.

She shivered at his touch. "I'm sorry I'm so nervous. I've never done anything like this before."

He smiled in the dark. It was funny she felt the need to tell him it was her first time. It was obvious she'd never been touched by a man in any way before. "I know." He leaned down and brushed his lips across hers again, but this time when his tongue flicked her lips, she knew to open her mouth for him. She kept a tight grip on the sheets to keep them pulled up to her neck.

Instead of trying to fight her over the sheet, he concentrated on kissing her doing his best to calm her fears. His hand stroked her cheek as his tongue tangled with hers.

After a moment, she relaxed her grip on the covers as she got caught up in kissing her new husband. She rolled to her side so she could move closer to him, not realizing what she was doing.

He took the opportunity to trail his fingers from her cheek down over the covers to her hip. He pulled her closer to him as he stroked her body through the layers of blankets.

His hand cupped her bottom and pulled her even closer so they were touching from chest to hips.

Emily felt a tingling all through her body starting from her lips and spreading down through her extremities. She'd never felt anything like it, but she knew immediately she liked it. How could he make her feel that way?

Benjamin pulled his lips from hers to brush them against her cheek. He'd missed being with a woman so much, it was all he could do to keep going slowly. "Are you cold?" he asked softly.

She pulled her head back for a moment, a little startled by the question. "No, not at all."

He smiled, and pushed all but the sheet off of her and down to the foot of the bed. "Good. We can get rid of some of these excess blankets then."

Her eyes widened as she realized she was now only covered by her thin white nightgown and a sheet. His hand slid under the sheet and stroked her from her shoulder to her elbow through her nightgown. "You're so small."

"Was Anna bigger than me?"

He nodded, not wanting to compare the two women, but he'd been unable to get his late wife off his mind. "Much. She was taller than Birgitta."

Emily was surprised to hear that. She'd never met a woman as tall as his sister before. She couldn't help but wonder if he wished she was a tall blond like he was used to. She didn't ask, though, she just looked at him in the dark with her wide blue eyes.

"I feel like you're going to break if I touch you," he whispered.

She'd been worried about that herself at first, but when he said it, it made her feel as if he didn't think she was good enough. "I'm not going to break. I'm strong." To show her courage, she lifted her hand and ran her fingers along his cheek, feeling the stubble there. She trailed her fingers down to his neck, and moved her hand around behind it to cup it and pull his mouth to hers again. She didn't know where the boldness had come from, but she liked his kissed and she wanted him to kiss her again.

This time when he kissed her, his mouth was more insistent against hers. She responded eagerly her tongue tracing the inside of his lip.

His hand moved down the back of her nightgown to her bottom, pulling her fully against him, this time with no covers blocking him. She felt his erection prodding her belly and pulled back in surprise. "It's normal," he whispered, pulling her back to him for another deep kiss.

He kept one hand curled under his head while the other slowly stroked her back, buttocks and thighs. After a moment, his hand came around to cup her breast through her nightgown. He was surprised to find it so full. She was so little, but she was perfectly proportioned. He wanted to remove her nightgown, but knew she wasn't ready for that yet, so he stroked her through the thin fabric.

She felt a pressure building in her center, and wondered if she was supposed to feel a sort of pain there. She couldn't ask him, though, so she just pressed closer to him, feeling strange as if she were doing something wrong when she felt him poking into her stomach.

He pushed against her shoulder and she rolled to her back, looking up at the blond head looming over her. His mouth dropped to hers again, and she moved her hands to his shoulders, holding on tight. It was then she realized he'd gone to bed without putting a nightshirt on. Did he always sleep without his clothes? Was he wearing his underwear or was he completely naked under the cover? She wanted to run her hand down his back to find out, but found she didn't have the courage.

He reached down and caught the bottom of her nightgown, bringing it up as he stroked his hand from her ankle to her thigh. He hoped he could convince her to stop wearing nightgowns altogether, but he didn't think it would be an easy task with his shy bride.

Once her nightgown was bunched up around her hips, he went to work on the buttons at the front of her gown. He knew there were at least three, but couldn't tell if there were more in the dark. He slowly unbuttoned the three he knew of and felt for more, never breaking their kiss. He didn't want to frighten her, but he needed to get her out of her nightgown so he could explore her fully.

She didn't realize his hands were on her buttons until he'd freed the fifth, and last, one and slid his hand into her open gown. His fingers cupped her breast and she let out a soft moan into his mouth. He toyed with her nipple, making it peak. "Your skin is so soft."

Her hands started moving as if of their own volition over his back, rubbing the strong muscles there. She marveled at the difference in their bodies. His was hard, where hers was soft. She could have laid in the dark touching him all night, but knew he'd want more from their wedding night than that.

His hands moved from one breast to the other touching her with his callused fingers. He was feeling more and more frustrated by her nightgown. Finally, he knelt at her side and helped her sit up. "Let's get this off you, sweetheart." He lifted her gown over her head and threw it to the floor pushing her back down onto the bed on her back.

She wanted to pull the sheet up over her body, but knew he had the right to see her and touch her any way he wanted. What was she thinking giving a man who must be twice her weight permission to do what he wanted with her? She felt the panic begin to rise again just before he lowered his mouth back to hers.

His fingers danced over her bare skin, along her stomach and breasts, before dropping lower and stroking his fingers through the triangle of hair shielding her innocence.

She jumped at the feel of his fingers there. Her mother hadn't mentioned he would do all this touching. Why wasn't he just consummating the marriage like her mother said he would? "I don't think you're supposed to touch me *there*," she whispered in embarrassment.

"Does it feel good?" His fingers drifted down and touched the nub hidden inside her folds. She jerked in surprise, but couldn't bite back a moan. "Does it?"

She nodded too embarrassed to talk about how he was making her feel. This had to be wrong, didn't it?

He seemed to read her mind. "Nothing that feels good, that we both like, is wrong for us. God made me to enjoy your body, and he made you to enjoy it, too. Stop thinking so much, and just enjoy what I'm doing to you." He covered her mouth in another kiss as one finger slid into her passage.

How was she supposed to stop thinking about it? Everything he did was foreign and strange and felt like she shouldn't be doing it with anyone, even her husband. When he started moving his finger in and out of her slowly, she got her answer. Suddenly all thoughts were gone, and she was just a creature of sensation. His movements felt so good. They made her feel better and want something more all at once. What was it?

After a moment, he added another finger, moving them in and out while his tongue did incredible things to hers. She wanted to scream at him to finish, but what was it she needed him to finish. Finally, she felt as if something popped inside her and all the tension left her as she rose her hips up toward his hand. He moved his fingers in and out a few more times, before rolling onto her completely.

He was braced above her on his elbows, his face seeming pained in the darkness. She stared up at him, uncertain what had just happened, but too relaxed to care. She felt something much larger than his fingers pushing against her, knowing it must be his man part her mother had said he would put inside her. She laid perfectly still waiting for him to hurt her with it, just like her mother had said he would.

He pressed it into her just a tiny bit, and it didn't hurt. It simply felt....strange. He pulled back and pushed in again, this time going further, but still not hurting her. Maybe he wouldn't hurt her at all. She relaxed a little as he pulled out and then thrust in hard, pushing inside her until he let out a loud groan.

She let out another moan, this time one of pain. It did hurt! She pushed against his shoulders trying to get him off of her. Her mother had said she needed to lie still beneath him and it would be over soon, but she didn't want to lie still. She wanted him to get off of her, and pull it out. "You're hurting me!" Her voice didn't sound like her own. It was breathless and held just a hint of a whimper. "Please stop!"

Benjamin groaned, forcing his body to remain still inside hers. "I'm sorry." He dropped a kiss to her lips, trying to help her find the passion again. He knew he wouldn't be able to remain still for long.

She kept pushing at his shoulders. She wanted to tell him to get off her, but she couldn't bring herself to be quite that rude. She lay under him instead, taking panting breaths, hoping he'd just stop and forget about doing this.

He stroked her cheek. "You're so beautiful. Do you have any idea how much pleasure you're bringing me?" He was determined to calm her and finish. There was no way he could pull out now, and he wasn't sure how long he could remain still.

"Really?"

"Really. Being inside you feels so good to me. I want to move inside you."

"Why?" She knew the question would show how little she knew about what they were doing, but she didn't care. He needed to understand she had to know what was happening to her.

He swallowed hard, trying to keep in mind how innocent she was. "Do you remember how good my fingers felt when they were moving in and out of you?"

"We shouldn't talk about that!" How could he bring that up now?

"Yes, we should. It felt really good, didn't it?" She nodded slightly, feeling the blush creep up her neck to her face. "Well, that's how this is going to feel, only better. You just have to get used to it."

"But it hurts!" she protested. How could he want her to let him do something that hurt her this way? Didn't he care that she was in pain?

"Does it still hurt?"

She took stock before answering him. "Not nearly as much."

"Good." He brought his hips back quickly and plunged back inside her. Her breath caught as she let out a slight squeal. "Did it hurt that time?"

"No. It felt...strange."

"For now, I'll settle for not hurting you." He kissed her quickly nipping her bottom lip. "Get ready for strange." He kept his movement slow and gentle as he moved in and out of her tight passage. It was obvious to him it didn't feel as good to her as his fingers had, but she was no longer protesting his movements. It had been so long since he'd been with a woman that he didn't last long. After a moment, he cried out and collapsed onto his elbows atop her. His breathing was harsh as he buried his face in her neck.

Emily lay beneath him running her hands up and down his back. She was glad she'd pleased him, even if she'd felt the act was lacking somehow. Her mother had promised her it would get better with time, and she hoped her mother was correct about that. Still, it hadn't been so bad she wouldn't be willing to do it with him again if he ever wanted to. She couldn't help but wonder how often he'd want to do it, though. Maybe once a month? Or less often? Her brow furrowed. She could handle it that often if he needed it.

After a moment, he rolled to his side, and reached down to drag the covers over both of them. They were hot now, but once the sweat on their bodies cooled, they'd be shivering in the cold. He lay facing her, not sure what to say now that it was over. What did one say to a wife he'd just met a few hours before after taking her virginity?

She rolled to her side away from him, snuggling into the blanket. She'd had so little sleep since his letter had arrived. Now that she was here, and the pressure was off, she fell asleep.

Benjamin was still trying to figure out what he should say to her when he realized she'd fallen asleep. Maybe flowery words weren't necessary for his little bride. He yawned and settled against the pillow, joining her in sleep. If they woke early enough, maybe they could enjoy one another some more before they had to go get the children.

∽

BENJAMIN WOKE EARLY, wondering why he felt so totally relaxed. After a moment he remembered and smiled. *Ahh... she's why!* He glanced over at the pillow beside his and saw his new bride sleeping with her head cradled on her hands. She looked even younger in his sleep, which made him feel a pang of guilt. She'd shown more passion than he'd expected, and he looked forward to further awakening her to the pleasures of the marriage bed.

He glanced at the clock he kept on the dresser and saw it was only half past six. That gave him plenty of time to give his new bride another lesson in love making. He smiled at the very idea. She may be tiny, but she was passionate, and he was thrilled with her pretty little body.

He leaned over and smoothed her hair away from her face gently caressing her cheek. When she didn't respond, he rolled closer, nibbling the side of her neck which was exposed.

Emily blinked as she felt a tickling on the side of her neck. She put her hand up to push away whatever was there and encountered a head. Startled, she yelped.

Benjamin chuckled. "Did you forget your husband was sharing your bed?"

Emily blushed. "Good morning." She couldn't admit to him that she had forgotten she'd married. She'd fully expected to open her eyes and find herself back home in her bed at her mother's house.

"Good morning, wife." He turned her toward him and dropped his mouth to hers to kiss her softly. "How did you sleep?"

"After four nights of sleeping on a train, I just slept. I don't even remember dreaming." She stretched her legs under the covers wishing she had the courage to stretch her arms above her head, but she knew she couldn't, because she wasn't wearing a nightgown.

"You nodded off pretty fast last night. I'm sorry you were so tired." His hand rubbed up and down her arm.

Her eyes met his before dropping again. Now that it was

daylight, she was too embarrassed to look him in the eye. "It was a long journey." How could she have been so brazen? Was she really not wearing her nightgown?

He brushed another kiss against her lips, his hands rubbing her shoulders. "We have an hour or two before we need to leave to pick up the girls." He pulled her flush against him, his erection against her thigh leaving her in no doubt about what he wanted to do to fill the time.

He couldn't really want to do *that* in the daylight, could he? He'd have to see her with no clothes on! "I guess I should fix breakfast then," she said trying to distract him.

"I have a better idea." His lips caught hers again, much more insistently this time. One hand cupped her breast and he flicked his thumb across the tip. His other hand rubbed her bare thigh, slowly slipping between her legs.

"Benjamin! The sun is up!" she protested. Surely he didn't really think she'd agree to have relations with him in the light of day. He had to know that was wrong!

He laughed. "The sun isn't the only thing up." He took her hand and brought it down to his erection, laughing as she pulled her hand away as if she'd been burned. "Let's make love." He pushed her to her back, his hand moving deliberately into her soft folds, trying to get her ready for him.

"We can't do this when it's light out." Her protest was softer this time as she tilted her head to the side to give his lips access to her neck once more.

"There's not a single scripture in the Bible that says it's wrong to make love in the daylight. I promise. I've looked." His probing fingers found her dampness and he smiled. No matter how much she protested, she was ready for him. He rolled atop her to settle between her thighs. "You'll like it a lot more this time."

She was startled at his abrupt movements and even more surprised to feel his male member pressing against her soft opening. As soon as he started to penetrate her, she closed her eyes, determined it was wrong to watch him while he did this to her.

He smiled at her shyness, but didn't stop moving within her. Now that he'd sated himself in her last night, he was certain he could last until she was finished this time. He wanted to see her face while she had her first fulfillment. He rocked in and out of her, reaching down to wrap one of her legs around his slim hips. She moved her other leg on her own.

He loved watching her face as she experienced the new pleasures. If she'd had any idea how wanton she looked, he knew she'd never allow him to touch her in daylight again. Her head moved back and forth on the pillow as she came close to achieving her goal, and finally, she arched her neck as her pleasure was upon her.

He thrust a few more times and finished quickly, content to collapse to her side and pull her into his arms.

She sighed happily, snuggling her face against his chest. "I really don't think we're supposed to do that when it's light out." She felt the need to make sure he knew how she felt about it, but she was too content to really complain much.

He laughed softly. "We won't do it during the day when the girls are here." He turned her face up to his for one more quick kiss. "Will that work for my sweet wife?"

She blushed but nodded. "I suppose it will have to do."

He rolled out of bed, unashamed of his nudity, and pulled his work clothes from the drawer. "Are you going to lie in bed all day, or are you going to fix my breakfast?" He fastened the buttons on his shirt as he watched her hiding herself under the covers.

"I'll get up in a minute." What she meant was she'd get up as soon as he'd left the room, and he knew it as well as she did.

He gave her a knowing look as he buttoned his shirt and took his socks and shoes from the closet. "I'll see you downstairs." He left, closing the door behind him.

She stayed in bed for a moment to make sure he wasn't coming back right away, and then jumped out of bed to scramble into her clothes. Emily smiled as she made the bed and straightened the room. Her marriage was off to a good start.

CHAPTER 5

After a quick breakfast of bacon and eggs, Benjamin and Emily drove out to pick up the girls. She was feeling extremely shy on the way out to his parents' house after everything they'd done together in bed. The silence was worse than talking though, so she asked, "Is there anything in particular you want me to fix for dinner tonight? Or do with the girls?" She stared straight ahead as she asked the questions, unable to look at him.

He thought about that for a moment, thinking the way she wouldn't look directly at him was adorable. "I don't care what you make for dinner. As long as I'm not eating my own cooking, I'll feel blessed." He squeezed her hand as he drove down the dirt roads through the countryside. "As for what to do with the girls, I'm not even certain what Anna did with them all day. Sure, I know she worked with them a little on their letters and numbers, and kept up with the housework. Maybe work with them on cooking and baking. Anna always said they enjoyed baking with her more than anything." He grinned at her. "And you could always spend some time working with Georgie on her housekeeping skills."

She smiled despite the sadness rushing through her. Every time he mentioned Anna's name, he said it with love. Someday, maybe she'd have his love as well, but for now she knew his late wife still had a firm hold on his heart. "I'll work with Georgie, and maybe we'll bake something. That's a good idea." She also decided she'd go through the girls' clothes and see if anything needed to be mended. It was never too early to learn basic sewing skills. "What time do you finish work for the day?"

"I lock the doors at six, but sometimes need to stay longer to straighten things up. I open at ten every morning. I like to eat lunch around noon or one, so if you ladies could bring something down for me, I'd appreciate that."

"Of course, we can." She wasn't sure what, because she'd had very little time to explore her new kitchen, but when they returned home with the girls, she'd look and see.

"Some days I'll want you to work for me so I can eat lunch in the back room, or I may ask you to help me stock the shelves, but for today, you need to just get acquainted with the girls and learn about your new home. And cook. You can't forget to cook."

She smiled thinking about his first letter. "Anything but bacon." She hoped they had a good store of food, because she liked to have options when she cooked. She'd had to work under Mrs. Walters for so long, cooking whatever was asked of her, that she loved the idea of having total freedom in the kitchen. She liked to cook whatever she was in the mood to cook and not have to follow a specific menu. She was truly looking forward to cooking for her small family.

He smirked pulling up in front of his parents' house and setting the brake. "Yes, anything but bacon." He paused for a moment. "We also need to get you some fabric so you can start making some new dresses for yourself."

He jumped down and helped her down to the ground

before leading her toward the house. He opened the door without knocking and called, "*Mor*? Abbie? Georgie? We're here!"

Abbie and Georgie came running followed by a straight faced Ingrid. The girls ignored their father and headed straight to Emily to hug her. "What are we going to do today?" Abbie asked.

Emily hugged both girls tightly. "I thought we'd start by fixing lunch," she told them. Then she lowered her voice as if imparting a big secret. "We'll bake some cookies and take them to your Papa at work." She raised her voice again. "We'll need to fix supper as well, of course, and someone needs to clean Georgie's room." Emily looked straight at Georgie as she mentioned her room, watching the little girl's face turn pink. "And we'll just spend time getting to know each other."

Abbie wrapped her arm around Emily clinging to her. "That's the part I'm looking forward to." Her eyes were full of excitement at the prospect of spending time with her new step-mother.

Benjamin watched his three girls talking together and sharing secrets. He turned to his mother. "I'm going to go out and talk to *Far*. Is he in the barn?" He knew harvest time was over, but his father would still never spend a lot of time in the house. His wife would drive him crazy if he did that, so he could usually be found puttering in the barn or spreading manure over the fields for extra fertilization this time of year.

"Yah. Go to the barn with him. Be off with you." His mother shooed him toward the door, making it clear that men didn't belong in her house during the day. After she'd shut the door behind her son, Ingrid turned to the girls. "Run along and make the beds you slept in last night girls. I want to have a little chat with your new *mor*."

Emily watched as the girls ran to the back of the big

farmhouse and turned to her mother-in-law with a smile. She hoped the woman was going to offer to teach her to cook Norwegian foods for her new family. It would be nice if she could cook them the foods they were used to eating.

"The first thing I want you to know is I do not believe my son should have married some woman he found through an agency. I had a delightful Norwegian girl all picked out for him who would have made him a good wife and who would have been a good mother to my grandbabies." Ingrid's accent was slight and musical to Emily's ears, whereas her new husband didn't have an accent at all.

Emily felt her face turn red and was unsure how to respond to her mother-in-law. She'd done nothing wrong, but the woman obviously hated her on sight for being someone who she didn't want her to be. "I'm willing to learn to cook Norwegian foods." She mumbled the words, knowing they'd never be enough for the tall white haired woman in front of her.

Ingrid shook her head angrily. "You can learn to cook the foods, but can you grow taller and look like a Norwegian woman? Can you change your family history so you will know our customs and our ways? Can you *become* Norwegian?"

"Of course, I can't, but I will do my very best to make your son and your granddaughters happy." Emily forced herself to keep her voice calm. She'd never in her life wanted to hit someone so much. How could her new mother-in-law be so ugly to someone she barely knew?

Ingrid clicked her tongue. "Oh, I saw how happy my son was this morning. Obviously you know some bed tricks to keep him satisfied, but he needs more than a woman to warm his body at night. He needs someone who will help raise his daughters correctly and who will help them turn into strong Norwegian women proud of their heritage. How can a tiny little woman without a drop of Norwegian blood do that?" She glanced over her shoulder to make sure the girls weren't coming their way to overhear. "It would be best for everyone if you got back on that train and went right back to the East where you belong before my granddaughters start to love you. Already little Abbie is calling you mama. You are not their *mor*! Their *mor* was a wonderful Norwegian woman who loved them. She does not deserve to be replaced with you!"

Her mother-in-law's words shocked Emily to the very core of her being. She'd been spoken to condescendingly, but had never lost her temper. This woman made her want to throw rocks. She'd come here planning to be the best mother and wife she could possibly be, and this bitter old woman had the audacity to tell her she wasn't good enough to be a part of her family? She struggled to keep her voice calm and low. "I'm sorry you don't like or approve of me, Mrs. Johnson, but I'm not going anywhere. I came here to be a mother and a wife, and that's what I'll do. I'm not going to turn tail and run back East simply because you don't think I'm good enough for your family." She walked toward the door, deciding to wait near the buggy. "Please send the girls out when they're ready. Thank you for watching them last night."

As soon as she'd stepped outside and closed the door behind her, Emily made a fist and slowly released it. How could someone be so close minded? If her mother-in-law thought Norwegians were so superior, she should have stayed in Norway! How could she move to another country, and not expect even one of her children to marry someone from that country? How could she condemn her without ever getting to know her simply because she was not exactly like her? Did she need to be a cookie cutter of every other person around her?

Emily desperately wanted to cry, but there was no time

for that. Her girls didn't need to see her cry, and Benjamin already thought she was weak. There was no way she was going to add to that thinking. She stood next to the buggy waiting for the girls to come out and join her. She had no idea how long Benjamin would be, but it had been eight when they'd left the house, and with an hour round trip, he wouldn't take more than forty-five minutes if he wanted to get back to town in time to open his store. She could stand there waiting all day by herself if she needed to.

∿

BENJAMIN WANDERED into the barn and found his father squatting down trying to hold a board in place while he hammered a nail into it. "Let me help, *Far*." He took the board and held it while his father swung the hammer as he'd done many times in his life.

"Enjoyed having the girls. You need privacy with your new wife you bring them on out anytime."

"Thanks, *Far*." His father, Sven, was a man of few words and always had been. Still, when something bothered him, his father was the first person he went to for advice. "It's odd being married to someone other than Anna."

Sven nodded. "I can't imagine being married to anyone but your *mor*. Especially someone so different from her. You went from a tall blond Norwegian woman to a tiny little thing with brown hair. Physically, they're as different as night and day."

"They're different in every way." Benjamin shook his head. "Emily is afraid of her own shadow. She's not much of a talker either. Anna never knew how to stop. If she wasn't talking, there was something seriously wrong with her." He paused searching for the right words. "I'm afraid I'm going to break my new wife in half every time I touch her." Not that it had stopped him, of course.

"You're going to have to be a lot more careful when you're with this one." Sven finished hammering in the nail and got to his feet. "Anna was a good wife to you, and I'm sorry she's gone, but you don't need your new wife to be just like her to have a good woman."

Benjamin considered that and nodded after a moment. "I know that, *Far*. She's just so...well...shy is the right word I guess." He chuckled for a moment. "My poor wife hasn't had the courage to look at me all day."

Sven gave a half smile. "Well, that'll work itself out eventually, I'm sure."

"She loves the girls already, though. I've never seen Abbie take to anyone the way she's taken to Emily. She's usually so withdrawn, especially since Anna died. I've been worried about her."

"Maybe it's good your new wife is a shy one as well. The two of them should do well together."

"If either of them can get a word in with Georgie talking nonstop all the time!"

Sven chuckled softly. "That girl sure is like her *Mor* and *Farmor*. She still talking herself to sleep at night?"

Benjamin laughed. "She does. I sometimes hear banging on the walls, because Abbie wants nothing more than to be left in peace and Georgie just can't seem to be content unless she hears the sound of her own voice."

Sven slung an arm around Benjamin's shoulders as they left the barn together. "You've got good kids there. Don't let anyone tell you anything different."

Benjamin spotted Emily and the girls standing next to the buggy as soon as he got outside. *Now why isn't Emily inside getting to know, Mor?* He walked over to the buggy and gave

Emily a questioning look. *Why does she look so sad all of a sudden? Is she missing home?*

"Everyone ready to go?" Benjamin asked, not asking the question that was foremost on his mind.

Emily turned to him and smiled brightly. "The girls and I are ready for our first day of getting to know each other. We can't wait, can we girls?" She smiled hesitantly at Sven. "It's good to see you again, Mr. Johnson."

"Oh, we're not so formal. Call me *Far*. Everyone else does." Sven patted her back. "We'll see you at church on Sunday. You take good care of my granddaughters."

"I will. I promise." Emily bit her lip to keep the tears in. He obviously didn't feel the same way his wife did about her joining the family. His kindness made it all the harder to hold back the tears.

Benjamin helped her into the buggy while the girls scrambled into the back. "See you Sunday!" he called to *Far*.

Once they were on their way back to town, he took Emily's hand in his. He wasn't sure what was wrong, but something had obviously upset her. When she was ready to talk about it, he'd be there for her.

Georgie chattered about how fun the wedding supper had been and what a good time she'd had at *Farmor's*. "*Farmor* let us help bake bread and I got to make mine into a face and put raisins in for hair."

Abbie made a face. "She put salt and pepper and sugar on it, too. It was disgusting." She leaned forward on the seat so she could talk to her new mama easier. "I put sugar and cinnamon on mine, and when it came out of the oven I put on just a little bit of butter. It was delicious."

"Mine looked better!" Georgie protested.

"But you had to throw it away. You couldn't even eat it!"

"I didn't want to eat it."

"Then why did you take a bite of it before you put it in the slop pail for the hogs?"

Georgie humphed. "I was curious, that's all." She suddenly spotted her favorite picnic spot. "That's where I like to go on picnics, Mama! Right over there by the pond."

Emily looked at the pond. "That does look like a nice place for a picnic. We need to make sure we take one soon before it's too cold." She'd only been on a couple of picnics. Her mother had always worked six days per week and did household chores on the seventh, so she only got to go when a friend invited her.

"Tomorrow?" Georgie asked.

"How about Sunday after church?" Emily suggested. She'd never driven a buggy before, and she didn't want to try without Benjamin there to help her the first few times. Besides, she liked the idea of having the whole family there when they went on their first picnic together.

"Oh, could we, Papa?" Georgie pleaded.

Benjamin smiled over at Emily, pleased she'd made the suggestion. "Well, if your mama wants to fix us a picnic lunch, then I'll be happy to eat it."

Georgie clapped her hands happily. "I can't wait. What will you fix for the picnic, Mama?"

"Hmm..." Emily acted as if she were considering the most important question she'd ever been asked. "I think I'll make some bacon sandwiches."

"But...you said you wouldn't do that when you wrote to us. You promised." Georgie sounded close to tears.

Emily laughed softly as she turned and smiled at her younger daughter. "I did promise. I was only joking. What do you girls like to eat on picnics?" She wanted to cook things they were familiar with eating, of course, and introduce new things as well.

"Mama...I mean our first mama used to just take bread

and some cheese and cookies and lemonade. Could we do that for our picnic, Mama?" Abbie asked.

"Of course, we can. We can take anything you girls want to take." She thought about it for a moment. "We can do some potato salad as well. Do you girls like potato salad?"

When there was no immediate response, Benjamin said, "I don't think they've ever had it. I know I haven't."

"Really? I'll make some. We'll see if you like some of the dishes I'm used to making." She looked at Benjamin. "Do you think Birgitta will teach me how to cook Norwegian foods? I really would like to learn so I can make you the things you enjoy."

He shrugged, wondering why she hadn't asked his *mor*. "I'm sure she won't mind. She's a good cook. Not as good as *Mor*, but she's good. It might be easier for her to teach you with how much closer she is, though." He eyed her speculatively. He really didn't care if he ate Norwegian foods or not. He was just happy to not be eating his own cooking anymore.

"Well, once I've settled in, I'll ask her to teach me. I do know how to cook a great number of things, so hopefully I can keep everyone happy until I've had a chance for lessons." She was suddenly worried about her cooking, which was odd. It was the one area in her life where she felt like she was truly accomplished.

Abbie leaned forward again. "I don't care what you cook, Mama. I'm just glad you're here with us."

"I am, too, Abbie." She squeezed the little girl's hand which was resting on the back of her seat.

Benjamin stopped the buggy in front of the house before helping Emily down. "I'm going to put the horses in their stalls and go straight to the store. Will you bring me lunch today?"

"Of course, I will. I may come down to do some shopping

as well. I'd like to see the store." She took the girls by the hand and led them to the house not nearly as upset as she'd been. The girls did wonders for her mood, and she was looking forward to her first full day with them.

Benjamin watched them go wondering again what had bothered her. He was glad she was happy again, though. It meant a lot to him that she wanted to see the store. He'd worked hard to make it what it was, and he wanted to be able to show it off to his wife. It was part of her life too, now.

CHAPTER 6

Once she and the girls were inside, Emily led them to the kitchen. "I know you girls want to do some fun things today, and we will, but first I need to get an inventory of exactly what we have in the kitchen so I can see what I need to get from the store. I want to be able to cook more than bacon sandwiches." She smiled at Abbie. "Do you know how to write?"

Abbie shook her head. "Mama was just starting to teach me when she got the fever."

"I'm sorry she died." Emily hated the sadness she heard in the girls' voices every time they mentioned their mother. She knew the sadness would eventually fade as they grew older, but for now, their mother's death was still fresh on their minds.

"We loved her a lot, but we're really glad you came to live with us," Abbie said.

The look on Abbie's face was sad, but hopeful as well. Georgie was off in her room re-making her bed and tidying up.

"I'm glad I came here too. I get two little girls and a

wonderful new husband." Emily thought about the best way to do things. "Would you run and get me a piece of paper and a pencil please? I need to make a list of what we'll need."

She opened the pantry door to see what she had to work with. There was a bin of rice, another of beans, a tiny amount of flour, and a bit of sugar. She sighed. She couldn't do anything at all with this. She was so glad the store was right downstairs. Abbie brought her the pencil and paper and she quickly started noting what she'd need. She couldn't make anything without more supplies. Even the beans would need some salt to make them taste decent and there was no salt to be found. She'd need to bake bread, and figure out what to make for a meal. She'd used the last of the bacon and eggs for breakfast.

By the time Georgie came down from cleaning her room, Emily had a list she could work with. She turned to the girls. "Do you want to go to the store with me? Or do you want to wait here?" She had to go immediately if she was going to be able to cook something for lunch.

Abbie stood up. "I want to go."

"Good." Emily smiled at her. "Come on, Georgie." If Abbie went, then Georgie had to go. Abbie was only six, but she could watch after her sister. Georgie was just too boisterous to be left on her own for even a few minutes.

Georgie followed along behind, chattering away about the fun things she wanted to do.

Abbie led the way through the house and down into the backroom of the store. "Papa likes for us to come in the back way and not use the street," Abbie explained as they walked.

Emily wasn't sure that would hold true now the girls wouldn't be going there on their own, but she followed along. As they rounded the corner from the back, she saw Benjamin carefully counting out change. "Come again, Mrs. Miller."

Emily waited until Mrs. Miller turned to leave the store before saying, "We didn't have enough food to do the cooking with, so I came to get some. I hope that's okay." She looked around the store in awe. She'd expected a small country store, but this was big enough to rival any she'd seen back home.

The shelves were lined with canned goods. Barrels stood in the middle of the store with beans, rice, flour, sugar, salt and many other staples. There were several different fabrics to choose from. Some had pretty patterns and some were simple, serviceable fabrics. Everything about the store impressed Emily. She was proud of what her husband had accomplished here.

"Of course. What do you need?"

She handed him her list which included a lot of staples as well as some meats. "I'm not sure exactly what you have here, so I just made a list of the things we need most."

Mrs. Miller turned around and looked. "Oh, is this your new bride, Mr. Johnson? I'd heard she finally arrived." Mrs. Miller looked to be in her late thirties. She was short and plump with laughing green eyes and brown hair.

Emily smiled at her and took her offered hand. "You must not be related to Benjamin."

Mrs. Miller laughed and shook her head. "His family only makes up about half the town. There are others of us here." She held up her shopping basket. "I need to hurry home and get started on lunch for my family. It was nice meeting you, Mrs. Johnson. I'm sure I'll see you at church on Sunday."

Emily watched bemusedly as Mrs. Miller turned and rushed from the store. She turned back to Benjamin who was filling up a crate with the things on her list.

The girls rushed over. "May we each have a piece of candy, Mama? Papa said we had to ask you." Georgie was, as usual, the one asking for them both, and Emily's heart went out to Abbie. She understood how hard it was to be so pain-fully shy. Emily noted the line of jars on the counter with different types of penny candy. Each jar held a treasure of candy for anyone with a sweet tooth.

"Just one each would be fine. I don't want you to spoil your lunch."

Benjamin added a bolt of cloth to everything else she'd asked for. It was a shade of sky blue that would match her eyes perfectly, and she loved it, but she was certain it was too costly. She knew instinctively he'd put it there for her to make herself a dress with. "Oh, that's so pretty, Benjamin, but something more serviceable would be better for me." She loved the color and the pattern, but she knew the cost would be dear.

He shook his head. "This is for you. My wedding gift." He looked her up and down, noting her old faded dress. "It will be beautiful on you."

"Thank you." She couldn't argue with him. It was his money, and he had to be proud of how his wife looked. If he wanted her to wear the blue, then she would wear the blue.

He lifted the box, and realized then how heavy it was. "How about you take just what you need for today with you, and I'll bring the rest home when I close up?"

She made a face. "I'm stronger than I look. You keep underestimating me." She lifted the box, which was heavy, but certainly not too heavy for her to manage. "I'll be down with your lunch just as soon as I get it cooked. It may be a little late." She would do her absolute best to get it ready in time, though. She didn't want to interfere with his regular schedule.

Once they were back upstairs, she put the things he'd given her away, noting the meat she'd asked for wasn't there. There was just a small portion of salt pork. "Where does your papa get meat?" she asked.

Abbie shrugged. "From the butcher. They trade."

"I didn't see a butcher shop." Of course, that didn't mean anything. The butcher could be outside of town, or he could simply be working from his home, where everyone would know to go with or without a sign.

"He's next door. He doesn't have a sign up. Papa keeps telling him he needs to get one so he can get more business."

"I see. Well, since we don't have meat other than the salt pork, I'm just going to make beans and rice for lunch. Is that okay with you girls?" She hoped they enjoyed simple meals like beans from time to time.

Abbie nodded, and Georgie said, "Yes, Mama. I'm not picky unless I have to eat bacon all the time."

Emily found a big pot and filled it half full of beans and added water from the pump. "I would rather soak them longer, but this will work." She set them on the work table and turned to the girls. "We need to leave those to soak for an hour, and then I'll boil them. Do you want to help me bake some bread while we wait?"

She spent the next hour working happily with the girls showing them just what ingredients to add to make the bread and how to knead it once it was mixed. Georgie wanted to make her own little pan again, so Emily agreed while she exchanged a look with Abbie. "Would you like to make your own as well, Abbie?"

Abbie nodded. "I want to make cinnamon bread like I did at *Farmor*'s. It was delicious."

"I think that's a great idea. As soon as the dough is done rising, we'll make the bread." She thought about the other things she needed to do to get caught up. As much as Benjamin's mother angered her, she was thankful the woman had kept them caught up on the major housework. She glanced at the clock on the wall. They still had thirty minutes before she needed to start boiling the beans. "We need to cut the salt pork for the beans. Do you girls know how to use a knife?"

She went to the work table and selected a knife for herself and two smaller, duller knives for the girls. Abbie's eyes widened. "Mama never let me use a sharp knife."

Emily wondered if she was doing the right thing, but she thought if she watched over them, the girls would do fine. "Well I'll show you how to do it, and you have to promise to be very careful. Okay?"

The girls stared at her with wide eyes. "I promise," Abbie said.

"I will be careful," Georgie told her.

She gave them each a small dull knife and stood one on either side of her at the work table. Georgie had to stand on a chair, but Abbie was tall enough to reach on her own. She gave them each a small slab of the meat and showed them the correct way to hold their knives to cut it. She demonstrated the size she wanted for the beans and they all stood cutting together. She did three fourths of the amount on her own, but the girls did some. When they were finished, she put it all in a small pile.

"Now we need to drain the beans and rinse them, and then we'll add water." The girls watched as she showed them step by step how to boil the beans. Then she started a pot of rice to go with them. "There. Lunch will be delicious." She walked to the table and checked on the bread, punched it down, and covered it again with a kitchen towel. She washed and dried her hands. "We have the ingredients for sugar cookies or a yellow cake. Which would you girls rather make today?"

Georgie started squealing jumping up and down. "Cake!"

Emily looked at Abbie. "Would cake be okay with you, too?"

Abbie looked at her sister and sighed. "Cake is fine."

Emily tilted her head to the side. "Do you prefer cookies?" Abbie didn't seem pleased at the idea of cake, and Emily wondered if she ever got to choose what she wanted.

"Yes, ma'am."

"Well, let's let your little sister choose this time, but next time you get to choose. Would that be fair?"

Abbie nodded a smile on her face. It was obvious that because Georgie was more boisterous, Abbie was used to giving in to her wants and needs instead of standing up for what she wanted.

"We'll bake the cake after lunch. We have about forty minutes before then, but I don't want to leave the kitchen with the pot boiling, because it might boil over. Would you each bring me all of your socks here? I know that's a silly thing to ask, but I want to make sure they don't need to be mended. We'll go through all your clothes today, and see what needs to be mended and what new clothes you need." Georgie made a face but ran up the stairs to obey. Abbie walked along slower, but she seemed to like the idea.

They each came back with four pairs of socks. Emily had never owned more than two pair in her life, so she was surprised they had so many. It showed her just how wealthy her new family was. She went through each sock and found Abbie had one pair that needed to be mended while Georgie needed every sock she owned mended. It made sense with the difference in the girls, though. George was certain to not be as careful with her things as Abbie was.

Emily had brought a small sewing kit with her and put it in the parlor where she was sure she'd be using it. She looked down at Abbie. "Would you run to the parlor and fetch my sewing kit? I put it on the table between the chairs."

Before Abbie could even respond, Georgie had run out of the room to do it. Abbie's face fell. Emily hugged the child with one arm, and said very softly, so Georgie wouldn't hear,

"Abbie, you and I are a lot alike. We're both quiet and shy. I know it seems like Georgie does everything first and always gets her way, but I'm not always going to let that happen. I'm here to watch out for both of you."

Abbie had a tear in her eye as she hugged Emily. "Thank you for being my mama."

She sat down with the girls and pushed the bread dough out of the way, showing them each how to carefully mend their own socks, before getting up to check lunch. By the time she'd done four of Georgie's socks, Georgie had done one and Abbie had done both of hers, it was time for lunch. "We'll put this aside for now. I'm going to take your papa his lunch. Do you want to come with me, or do you want to eat without me?"

Abbie stood up. "We'll come with you."

Georgie rubbed her stomach. "But I'm hungry!"

Emily looked at Georgie. "There's no one to stay with you since Abbie wants to come with me." After putting a large bowl of rice and beans on a tray for Benjamin, she held her hand out for Georgie. "Let's go."

They took the same path they'd taken before down the stairs and in through the back room. Once they were there, she stopped. "Should I take the food into the front, or just let your papa know it's here so he can eat between customers?"

"Take it to him, Mama. His customers know he eats while he works. They don't mind." Abbie led the way, so Emily followed.

She took the tray and set it on the counter behind Benjamin while he talked to a young woman in the store. Two older men sat in the corner playing checkers. One of the older men called out, "Is this your new wife, Benjamin? She's a tiny little thing!"

Benjamin finished with the woman and turned to the

83

men playing checkers. "Better to be a tiny little thing like my wife than an overbearing woman like your wife!"

Emily's eyes widened in surprise as she looked at the man to see how he'd react. Why would Benjamin talk to one of his customers that way?

He threw back his head and laughed out loud. "That's true. Very true." The man sniffed. "Your lunch smells good. Better than the bread your mother brings in even."

Benjamin put his arm around Emily's waist. "My wife is a good cook." He gestured to the man at the table. "The loud mouth over there is my cousin, Thomas. His friend is my brother, Samuel. They were both at the wedding, but I know you didn't have a chance to meet everyone."

Emily smiled toward the men and waved timidly. She felt like she was on display and she hated that. "Do you need anything else before I go back upstairs?" she asked softly. She wanted to hurry away so she could hide. She needed to feed the girls, of course, but getting out of the room was even more important to her.

"I talked to the butcher this morning. I got some chicken for our supper." He indicated a wrapped piece of meat on the counter. "Any day you want meat for supper, you tell me and I'll get it for you. We can have fresh every day with a butcher in town."

She nodded. "Thank you." She picked up the wrapped chicken from the counter and headed toward the stairs.

Benjamin caught her hand. "Are the girls minding you?"

Emily's face lit up at the question. "They've been wonderful. I don't have a single complaint. We're about to eat lunch, and then we'll bake some bread for supper."

His eyes searched hers. He'd worried a little that the girls wouldn't mind her because she was so little she wouldn't seem like an authority figure. "You would tell me if they didn't?"

"Of course, I would. Our girls are wonderful. They do everything I say." Both girls nodded to emphasize her words, and he let go of her arm.

"Okay, I believe you. You go and have a good lunch. I'll be home a little after six."

She picked up the chicken and hurried out of the store and into the back room, going up the stairs with the girls to have her lunch.

After lunch, Emily asked, "Do you girls like chicken and dumplings?" She'd always loved chicken and dumplings, and wanted to share the dish with the girls.

The girls looked at each other. "We've never had chicken with our dumplings, but we love dumplings. And chicken," Abbie told her.

Emily frowned. "Well, we'll try it and see then." The three of them made the bread. Each girl was given a ball of dough the size of her fist to make her own bread with while Emily made four loaves of bread and a dozen dinner rolls to serve with their chicken and dumplings.

As soon as the bread was in the oven, she began preparing to boil the chicken. Once it was on, she boiled the water to wash dishes. "Will you girls wash the dishes for me while I clean off the table and finish darning your socks?"

"You want us to do the dishes?" Abbie asked in surprise.

Emily wasn't certain what she'd said wrong. By Abbie's age, she'd been doing the dishes on her own. "Yes, would you wash so Georgie can dry?" After the girls were used to doing the dishes together that way, she'd have Georgie start washing. They were certainly old enough to learn to do simple tasks.

"We've never done dishes before," Abbie explained.

"Never done dishes? Really?" Emily went to the sink and put the bowls they'd used for lunch into it. "Just wash them until there's no food left, and Georgie can dry them. If you can't reach to put them away, set them aside and I'll do that."

She mixed the rice in with the beans for another meal, and covered the pot with the lid. She'd have to ask the girls how to get down to the cellar. She was sure there had to be one to keep the food cold, so they could store it for the next day.

She darned the last of the socks while the girls washed the dishes. She was glad they were so eager to help, even when it wasn't something they normally did. They talked back and forth as they worked together, somehow not realizing she was listening.

"Mama never made us do dishes," Georgie said, a slight whine in her voice.

"Well, our new mama says we have to do the dishes so we have to do the dishes. We're older now, and we can do them." Abbie's voice was patient while she explained how she thought things should be.

"Do you think we'll have to do them *every* day?"

"Maybe even after every meal, but that's okay. She can cook!"

Georgie agreed reluctantly. "That's true, but dishes aren't any fun."

"If they're not fun for us, then they're not fun for Mama either. Don't you want her to be happy here? We need to do some of the things that aren't fun to make her happy."

Emily bit her lip to keep from laughing. She honestly didn't mind doing the dishes, but the girls were certainly old enough to learn how and to start doing them on their own. Part of her job with her new family was to teach the girls to be good wives when they married. That meant teaching them to sew, cook, clean and do the dishes.

She finished up Georgie's last sock as the girls finished the dishes. Then she went to check on the bread. It was perfectly browned, so she pulled it out and dumped it on a cloth on the table. The girls looked at their own small pieces of bread. Abbie's was again pretty and smelled delicious. Georgie's looked like she'd rolled it in mud.

"Can we eat them now, Mama?" Abbie asked. "They'll be better warm."

Georgie frowned down at hers. "I don't think mine's going to be good warm or cold."

"Yes, you can eat them warm." Emily handed Georgie a dinner roll she'd put butter and a little cinnamon and sugar on. "Now you can eat something that tastes good too. Next time, don't put pepper on it."

Georgie smiled and bit into her roll. "Thank you, Mama!"

Emily checked the chicken boiling in a pot on the stove and decided to give it a little more time. She wanted the chicken to fall off the bone before she added the dumplings and made a gravy for it. "After you're finished, would one of you girls show me how to get to the cellar?"

"We both will," Abbie told her. "There's a little food down there, but not much. Mama usually kept a kitchen garden and canned in the fall, but she died and the garden was overrun with weeds." She made a face. "I kept telling Papa I'd grow the plants, but he didn't want me to."

Emily stroked her hand over Abbie's head. "We'll plant a garden together in the spring, and you girls can help me weed it, and then we'll can them all next fall."

Abbie's eyes met Emily's. "I start school in September." She looked down at her food, obviously nervous at the idea.

Emily smiled. "Before you start school, we'll make you two pretty dresses and I'll make sure you know how to read and write. It'll be easier for you that way." She certainly understood Abbie's reticence.

Abbie let out a sigh of relief. "It's not going to be easy anyway. I don't want to go to school."

"I didn't want to go either," Emily admitted, "but I made some really good friends there, and I'm so glad I did. It was hard, because like you, I'm really shy about talking to strangers. Will you have any cousins in school?"

Abbie nodded. "Lots and lots."

"That'll make it easier. We have almost a year before you start, though, and we'll have everything ready before then." She squeezed Abbie's hand to let her know they'd work together to get everything ready.

~

BENJAMIN CLOSED the shop a few minutes early, and headed across the street to the cemetery. He'd told Anna that Emily was coming, but he wanted her to know how good Emily was with their girls. He knelt on the edge of her grave and started pulling the weeds as usual.

"I got married yesterday. She's nothing like you. I guess in my head, I was sending off for a wife exactly like my first one." He set the weeds he'd picked off to the side. "The girls love her. She's very kind and gentle, and so far she seems to be a good cook. She's a tiny little thing, though. I feel like I'm going to break her if I touch her, and then I feel like I'm betraying you."

He sighed heavily. "I still miss you every day. I'm not sure how I feel about her, but I know she's making our lives easier. I'm sorry I had to marry her, but our girls, they needed a new mama. Abbie is finally smiling again. The first time she smiled after your death is when I agreed to send off for a bride. Now that Emily's here, she's smiling all the time. Emily's more like Abbie than you and Georgie. She's quiet. I have to work to talk to her, which I never had to do with you. I know it's strange, but I can't help but compare the two of you. I miss you, Anna." He stood up, still looking down at the gravestone. "I'll be late for supper if I don't go. I'll come see you again soon."

He turned and walked back toward the house. He hoped Emily had fried up the chicken, but whatever she'd done, he was certain it would be tasty. She didn't cook Norwegian, but so far, he'd liked everything she'd made.

He went into the house and washed his hands, inhaling the scent of the food she'd cooked. "That smells wonderful."

Emily smiled at him. "It's all ready. We were just waiting on you." She was nervous about serving her new family their first real dinner with her. Sure, she'd made him breakfast, but any idiot could make eggs and bacon. Beans were easy as well. Hopefully they'd enjoy the chicken and dumplings.

He looked around. She had made bread and it looked like there was a cake on the work table. His stomach growled, as he took his seat at the table. She served him a bowl of pieces of chicken and something else. There were sliced up carrots as well. He wasn't sure what it was. He looked at it for a moment, and then bowed his head to pray for his family.

"So what's this?" he asked, poking at it with his spoon.

"Chicken and dumplings. I can't believe you've never had it." Emily looked nervous that no one had ever eaten the food she'd fixed. It was a common meal in the East.

"So those white things are dumplings?" he asked.

"The girls said they'd had dumplings before. What do you think dumplings look like?" Emily bit her lip. No one had eaten a single bite of food yet.

"Well, usually they're darker." He noticed then the girls weren't eating and were waiting for him. He took a bite and was surprised at how good it was. "This is delicious." After another quick bite, he took a sip of his water. "You can make this every night!"

The girls each took bites and smiled. They obviously liked it, too. Emily breathed a sigh of relief and started eating her own food. "I can learn to make dumplings the way you're used to eating them if you'd like."

Benjamin shook his head. "Maybe, but I'll be happy to eat these any time you want to fix them for us." He reached out for a dinner roll and buttered it. After taking a bite he set it down. "Your bread is different from what we're used to as well, but it's very good. I guess food that's not Norwegian is good too."

Benjamin polished off three bowls and each of the girls had two. Emily had been planning to serve leftovers for lunch the following day, but she could see there wouldn't be enough. She couldn't complain, though, because they'd obviously enjoyed the meal.

Benjamin leaned back and patted his full stomach. "If you cook like that every day, I won't be able to fit through the door soon."

Emily smiled. "There's cake, too."

His eyes flitted to the work table where he'd noticed the cake earlier. "I'll hate myself later, but I'll take a piece of cake."

"Girls?" She looked to Abbie and Georgie to see if they were interested in a piece of the cake they'd helped her make.

Both girls nodded to indicate they wanted cake as well. She was surprised at how little the family talked while they ate. They seemed to take their food a lot more seriously than she was used to. She cut them each a slice of cake and returned to the table. She'd made a buttercream frosting for it she'd learned to make for the family she'd worked for.

As before, both girls waited for Benjamin to try it, and at his smile, they ate theirs as well. Emily took small bites of her cake while watching the others. Obviously she'd done well with the meal.

Finally, Benjamin pushed back from the table. "I know you said you'd worked as a cook, but when you said you didn't even know what Norwegian foods were, I doubted we'd be happy. I was wrong. This meal was simply wonderful."

Emily blushed, pleased with the praise. "Thank you." She turned to the girls. "Let's clear the table together, and then you girls can wash the dishes for me." She stood and began moving the dirty dishes from the table to the work table so they could be washed.

Benjamin watched as the girls helped her clear off the table, and then went into the kitchen to wash the dishes with no argument. He stared at Emily in disbelief when she joined him in the parlor a few minutes later. "How did you do that?"

Emily was confused. "How did I do what?" She hadn't done anything miraculous that she could see.

"Get them to do dishes so easily. I've been trying to get them to help with dishes ever since Anna died, but Georgie would start to whine, and Abbie would say she needed to calm Georgie down, so I would do the dishes myself. Every day."

Emily smiled. "I simply told them it was time they started doing the dishes and showed them how. They did the lunch dishes earlier." She dropped her voice. "I overheard Georgie complaining about having to help, but Abbie said they needed to do them to keep me happy, because she was sure I hated doing them, too." Her eyes were sparkling with laughter when she told him.

He laughed. "Yeah, right now, they'll do anything to keep you happy, because they don't want to go back to eating bacon sandwiches."

"I want to thank you again for the fabric. I'll start making a dress tomorrow. I didn't have time today with all the baking, and I wanted to get the girls clothes mended and see what they needed." She leaned against the back of the sofa, watching him out of the corner of her eye.

"Do you need to do a lot of sewing for them?"

She shook her head. "There was a bit of mending, but I got it all taken care of today. With the baking done and leftover beans for lunch, there's not even a lot of cooking to do tomorrow. I'll cut the dress out in the morning and teach the girls how to help me with it. I may be taking out their stitches and re-sewing after they go to bed, but at least they'll learn." She leaned back against the sofa and brought one of her legs under her, making sure her skirt was tucked around her modestly. "I also want to get started teaching Abbie how to read and write immediately."

"Why? They'll teach her that when she starts school."

"She's really nervous about starting school. She wants to learn early, because it will give her confidence." She hadn't known her letters at all when she'd started school, and most of the other kids had. She'd felt like she was way behind, and knew it would give Abbie confidence to know more than she had.

Benjamin frowned. "I didn't know she was nervous about starting school."

"Abbie and I are a lot alike. I remembered being scared to start school, so I talked to her about it." Emily shrugged. She seemed to know what Abbie was thinking and feeling most of the time, and she liked it that way. It made her job as a mother much easier. Of course, everyone knew what Georgie was thinking, because if she thought it, the words were soon coming out of her mouth.

"Well, of course, I want you to do what you can to make her feel better about it." He looked at her dress, hating how old and faded it looked, but not wanting to tell her that. He really wanted her to have her new dress done before he had her help him in the store or even took her to church. As a businessman, he knew he needed to keep up appearances.

"How long do you think it will take you to make your new dress?"

She made a face. "I know this one is awful, but I didn't have the money or the time to make a new one before I came out here." She thought for a moment. "If I spend a good amount of time on it every day, I can probably have it done by Saturday, I think."

He nodded. "Do that."

She blushed. "Do you want me to stop coming into the store until I have it ready? I can send the girls in by themselves with your meals if I need to." She didn't want to embarrass him, and she knew her clothes were appalling.

He could have kicked himself for bringing it up. "Of course not! Just finish it soon."

"Okay, I will."

The girls came into the room then, having finished the dishes, and the discussion was dropped. She'd hurry with it, though, because she didn't want to be an embarrassment to him.

CHAPTER 7

*E*mily worked as hard as she could on the dress for the remainder of the week. While she sewed, she had both Abbie and Georgie work on learning how to write their letters. By the time Saturday evening rolled around, they could both read a few simple words, and her dress was finished. She decided to surprise Benjamin with it by wearing it when he got home from work.

She was surprised with how quickly she'd taken to being married. She had known she'd enjoy being a mother to the girls, but she had been surprised by how much she'd enjoyed her time in bed with Benjamin. Just thinking about the time they spent together after the girls went to bed, she blushed. Benjamin could make her entire body sing with pleasure without even trying. With as often as they made love, she knew she'd be pregnant before long. She sometimes caught herself daydreaming about having a little boy or girl. She'd love to be able to give Benjamin a boy. She knew he loved his girls, but surely he'd be thrilled to have a son. Didn't every man want a son to carry on the family name?

She'd made pot roast for supper, and the girls set the table for her. They were getting to where she didn't even have to ask them to do the chores she'd designated for them. Even Georgie's room had looked tidy that morning after she was finished picking it up.

Everything was on the table and ready. She glanced at the clock and saw it was five past six. He'd be home any minute. She'd fixed her hair in a new way. She smoothed her dress down and straightened her apron. She was fidgeting and she knew it.

She filled each of their glasses with milk and took the pie out of the oven to cool while they ate. It was blueberry, which the girls insisted was Benjamin's favorite.

As soon as she set the pie on the work table Benjamin came into the room. He took a deep sniff and smiled appreciatively. "Every day I come home to new smells. You're spoiling me." He dropped a kiss on Emily's cheek before straightening up to study her. "Your new dress looks beautiful on you. No one is going to notice me at church tomorrow when I have such a pretty lady on my arm."

Emily blushed. "You don't have to call me pretty," she whispered. "I know I'm not." She knew pretty to him was blond hair. Short of wearing a wig, she would never have blond hair, so she'd never be pretty to him. She hated it, but she knew it was true.

His eyes widened in surprise, but he didn't respond because the girls were listening. They'd talk about it later. He couldn't let his wife go another day without realizing how pretty she was.

After the girls were in bed, she went straight to their bedroom as had become her habit, to change into her night-gown and braid her hair for sleep. Benjamin had gone outside for a brief walk as he did every night, while she readied herself. She knew he didn't really want to walk so late at night, but was thankful for the time he gave her to prepare herself for bed.

She stripped off her new dress and hung it lovingly in the armoire. She would happily wear it to church the following morning. She'd never owned anything quite so fine, and was very proud of it. She put her nightgown on and slipped between the sheets, knowing Benjamin would be back soon. She was always careful to cover herself up before he came in. He'd only seen her naked body once, and that was the morning after their wedding.

Within a minute of her getting into bed, he opened the door and quickly stripped off his clothes. She turned her head before she could see him unclothed, and he got into bed with her without turning down the lantern.

"You forgot the lantern," she reminded him.

He shook his head, looming over her in the dark. "Tonight I want to watch you while I make love to you."

She clutched the covers to her chest. "Why?" She couldn't let him do that, could she? The other time he'd seen her it was because it was daylight. Surely it wouldn't be proper to leave the lamp lit just because he wanted to see her.

He brushed his lips across hers. "Because you're beautiful, and I like to look at you."

She shook her head. "No, I'm not. I saw the picture you have of Anna in your drawer. She was pretty. I'm not." Why did he keep telling her she was pretty, when he knew she wasn't as well as she did? He was ashamed of her in her old clothes, and she could tell. If she were pretty, he'd be proud of her whether she was wearing something new or not.

His hand stroked down her body, and he was thwarted, as usual, by her nightgown. "She was pretty in a different way than you are. She was loud, where you're quiet. Tall where you're petite. The two of you are as different as night and day, but that doesn't mean you're not pretty, too."

"No one has ever said I'm pretty before." She stared up at him and realized that wasn't true. "Well, my mother did, but she doesn't count."

He smiled as he pressed kisses along her collarbone. "Of course her opinion counts. The girls think you're pretty. I think you're one of the most beautiful women I've ever seen in my life."

She turned her head to the side to give him access to her body. His fingers went to the buttons on her nightgown, pushing it open. His lips quickly followed the V he created as his hands went lower, catching the skirt of her nightgown and pulling it up.

"I wish you'd quit wearing these silly things. Why bother when you know I'm just going to take them off?" His lips were making her tingle inside. "You'd save yourself some laundry if you just skipped them altogether."

He coaxed her into a sitting position and pulled her nightgown over her head, his eyes going to her breasts which were now bare for him. His lips brushed against her nipple taking one into his mouth to suck on it.

She moaned softly, caught up in what he was doing, but still self-conscious about the light. "Please turn the light off," she whispered. She was almost panicked at the idea of him watching her while they made love. How could he think it was okay to do that?

"But then I couldn't see how beautiful you are when I do this," he whispered as he slipped his hand between her thighs, finding her opening. "I want to see your face when you find your pleasure."

She blushed, but couldn't stop herself from responding to him. He rolled to his back and pulled her on top of him, straddling his hips. Her eyes met his filled with shock. What was he doing? They couldn't make love this way. Could they?

She looked down and saw his erection for the first time.

She was shocked to see how big it really was. How had that fit into her? It was a good thing she hadn't seen it before they'd made love for the first time, or she'd have been even more afraid than she already was. She reached down and took it into her hand, something she'd never done. It felt strange to her.

He let out a groan and she let go as if her hand was on fire. "Did I hurt you?" she asked.

He laughed quietly, shaking his head. "It felt good."

"But is it okay for me to touch you there? It's not wrong?" Her eyes met his as she searched for her answer. Surely she shouldn't touch him there.

"Nothing is wrong between us. We're married." He caught her hand and brought it back to his member, showing her how to stroke him to make him feel good.

She watched his face as she continued the motions after he removed his hand. She was surprised to see she could bring him so much pleasure. She moved her hand slowly, and then faster, watching his face to see what he liked best. After a moment he caught her hand. "Did I do something wrong?"

"Not at all. I just don't want to finish without bringing you pleasure."

"Finish?" She stared at him blankly for a moment, and then understanding dawned and she blushed. "You mean you could do that from my hand on you?"

He nodded, amused at her innocence. Even after almost a week of marriage where he'd done his best to tutor her in the ways of love, she was still incredibly naïve. "I want to be inside you when it happens."

She blushed, and started to roll off him onto her back. He caught her hips. "Where do you think you're going?"

"You said you want to be inside me. I want that, too." As soon as the words were out of her mouth, she clamped her hand over it. How could she have said something like that to him?

His hands lifted her hips and positioned her over him. "I want to see how you like it this way," he whispered. He pressed up as he put pressure on her hips to get her to move down. Gravity did most of the work for him, and within a moment, she realized what he was doing as he pressed deep inside her.

For a moment she sat stunned, unsure of what to do. She bit her lip, simply enjoying the feel of having him inside her. He flexed his hips upward, and she moaned. "That feels good."

He smiled. "Good. Move around. Do what feels good to you."

She stared at him in surprise. He wasn't going to control their movements? After a second, she leaned forward, putting a hand on either side of his shoulders to catch her weight. She moved her hips up for a moment and then right back down. He groaned and she was shocked by how much pleasure riding him this way brought her.

It didn't take her long to find her rhythm, and a few minutes later, they both found their release. She felt the sweat trickling off her body as she rolled to her side beside him.

He reached out to turn the wick down, and she snuggled into his arms with her head on his shoulders. She was too embarrassed to say anything, but she fell asleep with a smile on her face. Marriage was definitely to her liking.

～

SHE WAS careful to avoid his mother during church on Sunday. Georgie ran to her *farmor* hugging her tightly, but Abbie clung to her hand throughout the time before and after the service. She spoke with Birgitta and a few others she'd met during the week during her forays into the store, but mostly she stayed to herself, which suited her and Abbie just fine. She enjoyed watching groups of people; she just didn't enjoy being parts of those groups.

Abbie watched the other children playing, and Emily tried to encourage her to join them, but she would only shake her head. "I want to stay with you, Mama."

After church, they walked the short distance to their home to get the picnic basket she'd packed before anyone else was awake. While Benjamin hitched up the team, she went to get the basket and a quilt for them to sit on. The temperature was chilly, but it wasn't so cold they would be uncomfortable during their time outdoors.

She hurried outside to find the girls already in the buggy waiting for her. Benjamin took the basket before helping her into her seat, and then handed the basket to her. Once they were on their way, she turned to the girls. "Are you excited?" She thought, no matter how excited they were, there was no way their excitement could match hers. She'd always fantasized about having a life where she could go on picnics when she wanted to, and now she suddenly had one.

Georgie bounced in the seat clapping her hands, while Abbie sat like a little lady, but her face glowed with pleasure.

"I made some things that I had on picnics back east. I wasn't sure if you'd like them, but I hope you will." Instead of going with just the things they'd talked about before, she'd added several things she thought her new family might enjoy.

Benjamin glanced at her. "Anything you want to cook, I'm happy to eat. I've never met a better cook, and I'm including *Mor* in that. Please don't tell her I said that, though." He winked at her as he drove carefully along the country roads toward the pond Georgie had indicated she enjoyed.

Emily felt as if she'd just been handed the best compliment of her life. With the way his mother spoke to her about not being able to cook Norwegian foods, she was thrilled he liked her cooking so well. "I won't say a word." And she wouldn't, but she was thrilled to receive the compliment.

She and the girls spread the quilt out before she dug in the picnic basket. She let the girls "set the table" with the plates and forks she'd brought. She brought out the small flask of lemonade she'd prepared and gave the girls glasses. Benjamin sat watching the whole ritual with a smile on his face. It was as if they'd rehearsed exactly how they wanted to do this.

While the girls were seeing to the lemonade, she started pulling out their feast. First came the bread and cheese. She also pulled out potato salad and devilled eggs along with baked beans. So many typical American foods were new to them because of the tight knit Norwegian community they'd always been part of. She felt like she was constantly introducing them to foods everyone she'd ever known had eaten.

She left the cookies in the basket, knowing the girls would want to have them right away if they knew she'd brought them.

They all sat down on the quilt, and Benjamin said their prayer for them. She took each plate and filled it with some of everything.

Benjamin spent a minute poking at his food before opening his mouth and taking the first bite of baked beans. His eyes widened with surprise. "These are beans, but what kind? What do you call them?"

"Baked beans." She loved introducing Benjamin in particular to new foods. He always looked at them like they were some sort of foreign insect, but then he'd open his mouth and take a big bite, and his smile would tell her what he thought of it.

KIRSTEN OSBOURNE

"Delicious." He tried a bite of her potato salad and smiled. "We have something similar. This is your potato salad, right?"

She nodded. "Do you like it?"

"I love it." He looked at the devilled egg. "An egg, but you've added something to the yolk." He sampled everything quickly and pronounced it all delicious.

The girls quickly followed suit, enjoying everything she'd made. When they'd all stuffed themselves, she pulled out the cookies. They were simple sugar cookies, but she'd frosted them to make them special. Georgie and Abbie each ate a few, but Benjamin said he'd have to wait as he patted his stomach.

Abbie looked at Emily with admiration in her eyes. "Mama, I want to learn to cook like you do. I'm sure I can have my pick of all the men in Minnesota if I can cook half as well as you can!"

Emily laughed self-consciously, but promised she would be happy to teach her everything she knew. She sat back and pulled one last thing from the picnic basket. "I don't know if you've ever heard of this book, but I received this copy as a gift for Christmas when I was ten. It's become my favorite book, and I've read it over and over again." She handed the book to Abbie. "Do you think you can read the title?" While both girls could read a few basic words, Abbie had learned to read some more difficult ones, and Emily hoped she could decipher the simple title.

Abbie stared at the cover for a moment, glancing at her father, and obviously a little intimidated that he was watching her. "Lit..tle. Little. Woe..men. Little Woemen?"

Emily smiled. "That's very good! It's *Little Women*. Have you heard of it?" Both girls shook their heads so she looked at Benjamin.

"Never heard of it."

"Well, it's about four young ladies who are trying to get

by the best they can during the Civil War." She looked down at the book in her hands, which she had treasured for ten years. "If you don't mind, I thought I could read a chapter or two while we sat here." She looked from face to face, hoping they'd like the idea. She wasn't sure what they were used to doing on picnics, but she knew the girls enjoyed being read to, so maybe they'd like the book.

Abbie smiled. "I'd like that more than anything!"

"Yes, please!" Georgie agreed.

Benjamin smiled and watched as his wife opened the book and began reading to his mesmerized daughters. "'Christmas won't be Christmas without any presents,' grumbled Jo, lying on the rug." Her voice was soft, but fluid as she read through the first two chapters. Both girls listened intently smiling and frowning at all the right places.

Finally, when two chapters were finished, Emily closed the book. "We'll read some more another time." She opened the picnic basket to return the book.

"Oh, please, just one more chapter, Mama?" Abbie begged.

"I'm afraid I'm going to lose my voice if I keep going." She looked to Benjamin. "Would you care to read a chapter?" She'd never heard him read aloud and wondered how he would do. His deep voice seemed particularly suited for reading.

He held his hand out for the book. He'd found the story of Meg, Jo, Beth and Amy as fascinating as his daughters did. He opened to the third chapter and began to read.

While he read the familiar words, Emily studied him. He was a different man than she'd met that first day. He was more relaxed now, and much easier to be around. Even his relationship with the girls seemed to have changed in some way she just couldn't put her finger on.

This was her first chance to just sit and look at her new husband without worry he'd catch her. He was a handsome man, taller than any man she'd known back east. His hair was blond, and his eyes were the same deep blue of his daughters. They reminded her of paintings she'd seen of the ocean. His nose was straight, and a little large for his face, but to her, the imperfection only added to his good looks. She knew if she'd met him any way other than the way she had, she would have automatically dismissed him as too handsome for her.

Benjamin finished reading the chapter and calmly handed the book back to Emily. She put the paper she'd brought with her to mark the page into the book and put it back into the picnic basket. "Is there anything else you want to eat? If not, I'm putting everything up," she warned.

Benjamin reached out and took one of the cookies he'd skipped earlier and ate it in two bites.

The girls both shook their heads still full from all they'd eaten earlier. Emily packed up the picnic basket to be taken home. There was enough food left they could have it for a cold supper, which would be nice, because she was tired. They'd done very little except go to church and picnic that day, but she'd gotten up two hours early to fix them a feast for their picnic lunch. How would her new family react if she napped this afternoon? she wondered.

Once they were home, she realized it was already half past four. They usually ate around six, so there wasn't a great deal of time before supper. She sent the girls to the kitchen with the dishes from the picnic and sat down on the sofa with Benjamin in the parlor.

"You look exhausted," he told her.

She nodded. "I am. I got up two hours early to fix the extra foods for the picnic. I could have made them yesterday, but I wanted to finish my dress. I also wanted the foods to be a surprise for the girls." She felt like she needed to explain her tiredness away, because she didn't want him to think she was simply lazy.

"They were a wonderful surprise. You said in your letters you could cook, but I think we expected you to be able to cook like most wives can cook. You could open a restaurant."

She brushed the compliment aside. "It comes from practice. I cooked for a living so I was cooking every day of my life. I was bound to become good at it." She tried to be modest about the compliment, but inside she was bouncing for joy that he enjoyed her cooking so much.

He patted his lap. "Stretch out and put your head on my lap. Sleep for a few minutes before supper."

She nodded. "You don't mind eating picnic food for supper again, do you?" she asked as she curled up on the sofa with her head on his thigh. His hand rubbed up and down her arm as she closed her eyes and relaxed.

"I was going to insist if you didn't suggest it." He dropped a kiss onto her cheek. "Sleep."

She yawned. "I never nap." She was too tired to protest any harder though. She closed her eyes and happily sank into oblivion.

"You do today."

~

IT WAS dark out when Emily woke up. She jerked awake startled to find herself on such a small space. Benjamin's hand automatically rubbed her back soothingly. "I was about to have to wake you. We're all getting hungry."

She sat up and stretched. "Thank you for letting me sleep." She blinked to trying to force herself to wake faster.

"It was my pleasure." He traced her cheek with one finger. "The girls are upstairs playing quietly. I had them set the table, but we waited for you to eat."

"There was no need. Everything can be eaten cold." She felt badly they'd waited when they could have simply eaten without her. She hated that he'd made the girls go hungry.

He shook his head. "We didn't wait because we needed you to cook for us. We waited because we wanted the pleasure of your company with our supper." He stood up and called the girls. "I'll help you set the food out."

"No, you don't need to do that!" It was her job to get the food on the table. He made a living for them, so she needed to do her share as well.

"I don't mind. You've made my life so much better by being here." He opened the picnic basket and helped her set the different foods on the table.

The girls came running in. "You slept for a long time, Mama. We're starving!" Georgie took her seat and waited while Benjamin and Emily finished putting the food out.

Abbie sat down and folded her hands in her lap. "Did you have a good nap, Mama?"

"I did. Thank you both for being so quiet." Emily took her seat and waited while Benjamin took his. He prayed softly, before they each took a generous helping of everything left. "What time is it anyway?"

Benjamin grinned. "Seven thirty."

"But we eat at six! You should have gotten me up." She wondered why they weren't angry with her. There was no reason she should have slept so long.

"None of us will die from eating an hour and a half later than usual."

"I thought I was going to," Georgie complained.

Abbie kicked Georgie under the table. "We understood you were tired. We were happy to wait."

Emily looked at Georgie. "I'm very sorry I made you wait. I won't make a habit of it."

Georgie sighed. "I guess it was okay, but just this once."

After supper, the girls did the dishes without being told. Emily gathered the dirty laundry from the house and put it together to be washed and hung on the line in the morning. Once she was finished, she returned to Benjamin who was reading the small local paper in the parlor.

"I'm going to spend tomorrow doing laundry and baking, but if you want, I'll come into the store on Tuesday and you can show me around so I'll be ready to take your place if need be." She loved the idea of helping him with his work on occasion.

He studied her for a moment and nodded. "I'd like that. I also want you to pick out some fabric to make yourself two more new dresses."

Her eyes widened. "Oh, but I already have this new dress. I can wear this whenever I work in the store or go to church, and my old ones for around the house." She hated the idea of wasting money and time on more dresses for herself when there were so many things the girls needed.

He sighed taking her hands in his. "No, you really can't. I don't want to insult you, but your old dresses are much too shabby to wear around town. As the wife of the owner of the only store in town, you're expected to dress better than most women, and you don't dress nearly as well as most of the others. Please don't take this wrong, but you need a whole new wardrobe as quickly as possible."

She looked down at her hands embarrassed. "Well, one more dress would be enough then. I'll have one for dressing up and one for every day." How could she not have realized just how strongly he felt about her wardrobe? She could make another dress quickly.

"Two more is the least amount. I'd prefer you made another six dresses, so you'd have one for every day of the week. Don't worry about the money. I'm not a wealthy man, but I can certainly afford some new dresses for my wife."

She sighed. "I want to make the girls some new clothes, too, though. I don't want to spend all my time on my own clothes." She would feel guilty spending that much time on herself when she had two little girls who needed dresses as well. What she had covered her sufficiently, but the girls' dresses were getting much too short.

"Well, how about this? Make two more dresses for yourself, and then two dresses for each of the girls and then two new dresses for yourself again. I know it's a lot of sewing, but you really need the new clothes." He thought for a moment. "Or we could have *Mor* make dresses for the girls. She wouldn't mind."

Emily was offended at the very idea. "I'll stay awake sewing all night every night before I'll allow your mother to make more clothes for the girls. It's my responsibility, and I'll do it." She was certainly going to take care of the girls' clothes herself no matter what.

Benjamin was surprised. Anna would have jumped at the chance to ask for help. "Why?"

"Your mother already thinks I'm not good enough to raise your girls. I'm not going to give her more reason to hate me." Emily knew her voice sounded angry, but she didn't know how to change that. His mother was hateful to her, and she was simply not going to give her reason to act the way she already did.

"*Mor* doesn't hate you!" He knew she was annoyed that he had married someone from out East instead of Kristen, but she didn't hate Emily. Mor didn't hate anyone. "She's just not used to the idea she doesn't get to do everything for the girls anymore. She liked having them under her control."

Emily knew it wasn't the truth, but she wasn't going to argue with him. "That must be it." She wasn't going to discuss it any longer so she quickly changed subjects. "I'll come by the store in the morning and pick out more fabric. I can have another dress made by the end of the week if I start right away." And she would. If it killed her she'd have both dresses done by Sunday, and then she could start on new dresses for the girls on Monday of the following week.

After making love that night, she lay in her husband's arms thinking about their day. Other than their slight argument about her dresses and his mother's help, it had been a good day. She'd dreaded going to a new church for the first time, but she'd been pleasantly surprised by how well that had gone. It was nice to have Abbie at her side while Benjamin was off talking to friends and relatives.

"I want to thank you for how accepting and loving of my daughters you've been," he told her as he played with her hair. "You've made it very clear to them that you love them and consider them your own. I can't think of another woman who would have been more perfect for the job of being mother to them."

She blushed in the dark. She was thankful for his words of praise, but wished he would tell her she'd been a good pick for wife for him as well as mother to the girls. "I enjoy the girls a great deal. I love them both as if I'd given birth to them." She had been surprised at just how much she loved the girls. She knew she enjoyed children, of course, but she didn't expect to love the two of them as much as she did.

He kissed the top of her head. "It shows in the way you treat them. Abbie especially has been a completely different child since you've been here."

"Abbie is a joy for me. I understand how she thinks because we're so much alike. Georgie is a delight as well, but I don't feel the same affinity for her. Not that I don't love her as much, I just don't quite understand her." It wasn't as important for her to understand Georgie, though, and they both knew it. Understanding Abbie was the important thing, because Abbie was quieter and not as given to sharing her feelings. Georgie was happy to tell a total stranger what she thought and felt about any subject under the sun.

He laughed. "I don't think anyone truly understands Georgie. She's a boisterous child."

"I think you sending off for a wife when you'd so recently lost one must have been a difficult thing to do. It shows just how much your girls mean to you. You can't be with them all the time, because you need to support them, so it made sense you provided them with someone who could be with them all the time." She brushed her lips across his bare shoulder. "I'm just thankful I was the one who got to complete your family. I think I'm going to be very happy here." She already was happy. If she had his love, though, her happiness would be complete. She couldn't tell him that, though.

As the thought occurred to her, she realized the truth. She'd fallen in love with her husband. How could she have gone and done such a thing? He was still in love with his dead wife. He only praised her about being a good mother, not about being a good wife to him.

Why did the knowledge of being in love with her husband make her suddenly feel so lonely? Why couldn't she simply accept what he had to give her? He shared his life with her. Shouldn't that be enough? She hadn't come here wanting or expecting love from him. It had been an arrangement to help him with his girls and so she would have a home to go to at the end of the day. He'd done everything he'd said he would do for her, and she should be happy with that. Why wasn't she?

She rolled away from him and faced the wall, curling into a ball. Being in love should fill her with joy, shouldn't it? So why did she feel like she would never feel warm again?

CHAPTER 8

*E*mily and the girls went to the store with Benjamin on Monday morning to pick out the fabric for Emily's two new dresses. Emily decided she'd cut them both together, so she could save some time. She looked through the different bolts of fabric trying to check the prices without Benjamin seeing her. He'd told her to pay no attention to the price, but she just couldn't force herself to ignore the prices. She'd had to live frugally for too many years to give up the habit now.

The least expensive cloth was a dark brown. She didn't particularly care for it, but she could make a good serviceable dress from it. She held it up and studied it for a moment.

From across the room, Benjamin saw Emily hold up the ugliest fabric he'd ever seen. It was the least expensive fabric he had, so he knew what she was doing. Why couldn't she listen to him when he told her she could have any of the fabrics in the store without a problem? He strode across the room and removed the fabric from her hands. "I'll pick your fabrics."

"But..."

111

"Absolutely not. You will not nickel and dime your wardrobe and wear ugly dresses." He ran his finger along the tops of the different fabrics, trying to find the pastel colors he knew would be best on her. Finally his fingers found the pink he'd been looking for. He held it up in front of her, judging the color. "This one." He handed it to her to hold while he found the other color. He stopped on a mint green, again holding it up to her face. "And this one." He put the brown back in its former place. "Those will look the prettiest on you. I'll watch when I get the next shipment in for more pretty colors."

"You can't always give me the best of the shipments, Benjamin. You'll lose business." She couldn't stand it if he were to lose money because of her.

"It's my business to lose. No more ugly dresses for my wife!" He walked to the counter and picked out a cameo brooch he'd had his eye on for her, and plucked it from its display. "You'll take this as well, and you'll like it!" His eyes dared her to argue with him.

She took the things he handed to her. "Thank you." Why did she feel so annoyed with him for giving her pretty things? "I'll go get started right away." She was halfway up the stairs with the girls when she realized why she was angry with him. It was because he was ashamed of her. Her steps slowed as she blinked back tears.

Straightening her shoulders, she hurried up and sat down at the table. She'd gotten up early to do her baking and laundry, so now the only thing left was to do her daily cooking. Lunch was on the stove, so it was just a matter of getting the sewing done. "Are you girls ready to see just how fast we can make two dresses?"

Abbie smiled and nodded. "I think we can have them done by Thursday, Mama."

"I hope so, because I want you each to have a new dress

by Sunday as well." No matter what it took, she was going to have the dresses Benjamin insisted she needed and the dresses the girls needed done by Sunday. She didn't care if she got no sleep before then.

~

WITH CAREFUL CUTTING, she was able to get a dress for herself and a dress for each of the girls out of each of the bolts of cloth. She even had enough left over to make them matching bonnets. When Sunday morning dawned, all three of them were in new dresses. She'd stayed up late into the night to finish the dresses for the girls despite Benjamin's protests. If he was embarrassed of how she dressed, how could he not be embarrassed of the girls' too-short Sunday dresses? She wouldn't embarrass him again.

She put her brooch on to finish off her pink dress and walked down to walk with her family to church. They'd been invited out to Benjamin's parents' house for lunch after church, and she was not looking forward to going. She knew it would be a little easier with the work she'd done all week proudly displayed on herself and the girls, but she was sure her mother-in-law would find something to complain about.

After church, she followed Benjamin out to the buggy and climbed in beside him. She'd made some dinner rolls and a side dish to take with them, hoping her mother-in-law would appreciate the gesture.

When they pulled up into the yard, she realized they were the only ones there. Why had she assumed it was going to be the entire extended family? She didn't want to be alone with her mother-in-law for any period of time. The woman spewed venom at her anytime Benjamin wasn't there.

Benjamin helped her down and she carried the dinner rolls and Benjamin carried the pot with her corn chowder into the house. Even though they weren't Norwegian foods, she hoped that the fact she'd made an effort to help out with the meal would be appreciated.

Georgie ran in and hugged her *farmor*, while Abbie hung back clinging to Emily's hand. Emily set the dinner rolls she'd made on the work table and Benjamin put the corn chowder down as well. The corn chowder had been kept warm in the oven while they'd been in church, and they'd picked it up on their way to the farm.

Ingrid thanked Emily for the food and smiled at her. Emily wasn't sure what brought about the change of heart, but she was thrilled to see it. She helped set the table and put the food on while everyone settled into their seats.

Benjamin's father said the blessing and as soon as they were done, and the food was served. Emily couldn't help but notice that everyone ate some of the food she prepared except Ingrid. Sven complimented her on the corn chowder. "This is a soup? It's very good!"

"It's corn chowder. It's a very popular dish in Massachusetts." Emily ate a bit of everything. She watched as the girls ate some of everything, but had seconds of the corn chowder. She couldn't help but smile over the way they devoured the new foods she fixed them.

After they were finished eating, the men went out to the barn, while she stayed inside with Ingrid and the girls. She helped clear the table, and watched as the girls automatically helped as well. She was pleased the girls were doing what she expected of them at home even when they were at their grandmother's house.

When it was time to start the dishes, Ingrid shooed the girls outside to play. Abbie bit her lip and looked at Emily uncertainly, but Emily nodded. "Run along. We'll do the dishes."

As soon as the door closed behind the girls, Ingrid turned

on Emily. "You are ruining those girls! Why did they think they needed to help clear the table? At my house they're still little girls, and they don't help with cooking or cleaning. And the food you prepared? Why haven't you learned to cook anything Norwegian yet? My son prefers Norwegian food and you must be a huge disappointment to him. I don't know why he hasn't sent you right back East where you belong!"

Emily blinked a few times at the about-face. She should have expected it, but she hadn't. "I'm not going to fight with you, Mrs. Johnson. I'm doing the best I can do with the girls, and I'm cooking what I know how to cook. They aren't starving under my clumsy attempts to feed them, so I must not be doing too badly!" She bit her tongue against what she really wanted to say. She'd never used a swear word in her life, but she wanted to then. She mentally counted to ten, and then repeated it.

"How dare you talk to me that way? In the Norwegian culture we respect our elders and treat them as if they are wiser."

Emily slammed down the dish she was drying, turning to face her mother-in-law. Where she got the courage, she would never know, but she wasn't going to put up with being treated badly for another minute when she had been working her fingers to the bone for her new family. She simply hadn't had enough sleep to deal with her mother-in-law. "As you've pointed out repeatedly, I'm not Norwegian! I respect people who treat me as if I'm a human being. Since you can't see fit to treat me as if I'm better than an animal, I feel no need to treat you with respect." She threw down her dish towel and stormed outside, leaving her mother-in-law to do the dishes on her own.

She found the girls sitting on the ground playing with marbles. She squatted down to join them, fighting against her anger. The girls didn't need to see her have an angry fit, whether she wanted to or not.

She took deep calming breaths as the girls explained the "rules" for marbles, and she watched them play with a smile. Her own childhood had included few games of fun, and she enjoyed watching the girls play. Within minutes she'd calmed down again, although she was determined to speak with Benjamin when they got home about the way his mother treated her. She was thankful the woman hadn't chosen to attack her in front of her girls, but she still wasn't pleased she'd been attacked at all.

~

BENJAMIN LEANED against the horse's stall in the barn while his *Far* smoked his pipe. "I'm really surprised at what a good little wife she is. The girls absolutely adore her, and she's helped Abbie to come out of her shell. I never thought I'd see Abbie smile again after Anna died, but Emily has brought about a miracle. She's laughing and smiling again, and reading! Emily has taught her to read beautifully in just two weeks. My house is like a different place." Benjamin couldn't say enough good things about his new wife. She'd been a true blessing to his family, and he was ready to put a halo on top of the tiny woman's head.

Far nodded, listening. "And you're not afraid to touch her anymore?"

Benjamin laughed. "I got over that. I honestly never thought I'd be able to have another woman in my life after Anna, but Emily has completed our family." He patted his stomach. "And her cooking? I've never tasted anything like it. At first, I was disappointed that she didn't know how to make any Norwegian dishes, but I find I don't miss them at all. Every day she makes something I've never had before and

I like it more than the last thing." He pulled out the waist of his slacks. "I had lost a lot of weight after Anna died, and I've put it all right back on since Emily got here. She's going to have to let the waist out on all my pants in another week if I keep eating the way I have been!" He knew he was raving about her like a man in love, but he just couldn't seem to stop himself.

"The corn chowder was delicious."

"Everything she cooks is delicious. And she sews beautifully." He didn't add that she kept him happy in bed as well. He knew his *far* could see that written all over his face.

"I noticed the three of them wearing matching pink dresses today."

Benjamin smiled as he thought about their outfits for church. "I have to fight her to spend money on herself. She looks for the least expensive thing trying to save every penny she can. I have to fight her to get her to take more expensive things." He sighed. "I wish she was willing to spend just a bit more on herself, but at least she's not trying to spend every dime I make on frivolous purchases. What kind of man complains that his wife doesn't spend enough?"

Far just nodded.

"She has so much patience with the girls. There are times when I'm getting frustrated with Georgie, and she'll just smile and talk to her softly, correcting her behavior without Georgie even realizing it. And the girls now do the dishes after every meal without even being asked. They wouldn't do them for me for anything, but they'll do anything for Emily." He leaned back against the wall of the barn, smiling and staring off into space as he spoke.

"I'm glad you found a woman you could love."

Love? Was he in love with Emily? Surely not. He stood staring at his father for a moment in stunned silence. He appreciated Emily, of course. And there was no doubt he felt desire for her. He proved that over and over again. But love? Wasn't love the overwhelming feeling he'd always felt for Anna? He remembered sitting in the schoolroom staring at Anna, and walking her home after school stealing a kiss.

Was that just schoolboy love? Was he feeling an adult love for Emily? He'd never questioned how his love for Anna had changed during their years of marriage. She'd just been there for him. Had love for his new wife crept up on him without him even realizing it?

"I don't know that I love her, *Far*." He couldn't love her. He'd promised Anna he wouldn't fall in love with his new wife.

Far laughed. "You don't, huh? You stand there moon-eyed talking about the woman non-stop and you don't think you love her? Of course, you do. You think the woman can do no wrong. You've done nothing but praise her since we came in here. Tell me, how would you feel if Emily left?"

Benjamin felt a sinking feeling in his stomach. How would he feel if Emily left? He'd hate it. How could he love her, though? He'd vowed to love Anna for the rest of his life. Or the rest of her life. Anna's life was over. Did that mean he had the right to move on and love another? Could he love another?

He gave *Far* a blank look.

Sven clapped his youngest son on the shoulder. "You think about it. She's a lovely young woman, and I'm happy she's in your life. She's exactly what you needed now that Anna is gone." He sighed softly. "I know you think you buried your heart with your wife, but you're too young to do that. You have a wife who is making you feel whole again. She's healing your heart and the hearts of your children. Let yourself love her."

The two men left the barn and Benjamin frowned when he saw his wife crouching in the dirt with the girls. Why did she never stay in the house with his *mor*? He knew she was shy, but *Mor* was family, and she deserved to be treated with more respect than that. He'd have to talk with her about it when they got home.

Emily looked up when she saw Benjamin approaching with his father. "Are you ready to go?" she asked.

He nodded. "Are you?" He looked around in confusion, wondering if his mother had come outside with them or if she'd stayed in. Why did Emily always leave her alone?

"Yes, but I forgot the bread basket and the pot with the chowder in the house. Would you mind getting it for me?"

He gave her a questioning look, but she shook her head, indicating the girls. She obviously had something she needed to say to him without the girls listening. Whatever it was could wait until he'd talked to her about her disrespect for his mother, though.

He went into the house and said goodbye, getting the pot and the bread basket. "We'll see you at church on Sunday, *Mor*." He pressed a kiss to her cheek as he took the things he needed.

She smiled at him brightly. "I do miss seeing the girls. I don't feel like I can go visit them during the week since Emily hates me so much."

Benjamin's eyes widened. "Emily hates you? What do you mean?" Hadn't Emily told him his *mor* hated her? What was going on?

She had tears in her eyes as she said, "She actually told me she doesn't respect me. Her culture must be a great deal different than ours."

"I'll talk to her, *Mor*. She can't treat you that way." He shook his head. Emily was obviously very different around his mother than she was around him. "You can come into town and see the girls anytime you want during the week. I won't let her stop you." He was angry at the mere idea of

Emily trying to stop his mother from seeing the girls. What was she thinking? Yes, she was their new mother, but they had every right in the world to see their grandmother.

His mother smiled and hugged him. "Thank you, Benjamin. I'm so glad you respect me, even though your wife doesn't."

He carried the things out to the buggy, handing them up to Emily who must have been helped in by his father. He was so angry with her he couldn't speak as they drove home. How could she treat his mother so disrespectfully?

Once they were home, he helped her down from the buggy without saying a word. While he unhitched the horses, she took the girls inside, and sent them upstairs to play in their rooms. She had to talk to him about the way his mother was treating her.

She heard the front door slam behind him and waited for him in the parlor. He walked in and looked around. "Where are the girls?" He didn't want them to hear what he had to say to her.

"I sent them up to their rooms to play. I need to talk to you." Her face showed her anger over something. He wondered what right she had to be angry when she was the one mistreating his mother.

"Good. I need to talk to you as well." He took a deep breath, still trying to control his temper. "*Mor* told me you said you didn't respect her." He waited for her to deny it, so he could yell at her for lying. He was so angry all he wanted to do was yell at her. How could she be so different with him than she was around his mother?

She felt her heart drop into her stomach. "Excuse me?"

"She was in tears. Why do you always leave her house when I'm talking with *Far* in the barn? Why don't you stay in the house and help her with dishes like all my sisters do? Like Anna did?" He felt guilty for throwing Anna in her face, but she'd said she didn't respect his mother. What kind of woman said that to her mother-in-law?

Emily closed her eyes and took several deep breaths. She couldn't believe she was being accused of wrongdoing when she had been the one mistreated. "May I tell you what happened without interruption please?"

He walked to her and sat next to her on the sofa. His movements were angry, and she knew he was furious with her. "Be my guest. I'll listen." And he would try to listen. He wasn't sure he could, but he would try.

"After lunch the girls helped clear the table like they do at home, and they were going to help with the dishes. Your mother sent them outside instead. She told me I'm ruining the girls by making them help with dishes, and that I need to cook Norwegian foods for them. She complains to me I'm not Norwegian every time I see her." She felt the tears sting her eyes as she recalled how his mother had treated her. "She told me I'm a huge disappointment to you. I explained that I cook what I know how to cook and the girls aren't starving, so I must be doing okay. She told me that in the Norwegian culture people respect their elders. I told her I don't respect people who treat me worse than they treat animals, and that's exactly what your mother does. She's very cruel to me."

Benjamin clenched his fist. How dare she try to blame his mother for her cruel words? "She wouldn't have said that to you. She may have suggested you learn to cook a few Norwegian meals, but the rest of it? I don't believe it. *Mor* was always kind and loving to Anna. Why would she be any different to you?"

"Because I'm not Norwegian and I disappoint her? How should I know? I only know how she treats me, and I don't like it! I can't believe you believe her over me. Have you ever known me to be unkind to anyone?" She stared at him in disbelief. She was his wife, and she'd done everything he'd asked of her and more. She had never done a single thing to upset him, and he believed that old harridan over him? What was wrong with him?

"No, but I've never known *Mor* to be unkind either, and I've known her far longer than I've known you."

Emily recoiled as if she'd been slapped. She'd really thought her marriage was a good one until today. "I see." She stood up and went into the kitchen to start the evening meal.

He followed her. "You will promise me to be kind to my mother."

"Yes, of course, I will." She removed the iron skillet she needed to brown the potatoes she planned on frying from the wall not looking at her husband. As far as she was concerned, until he started to believe her, their marriage wouldn't work.

Benjamin stood staring at her back, wondering why she'd stopped talking to him. Finally he threw his hands up in disgust, leaving the house and slamming the door behind him.

As soon as she heard the door close, Emily sat down at the table and put her head in her hands and cried. How could she fight a dead wife and a mother-in-law who hated her? She'd lost her husband, and she knew it.

IT WAS ALMOST DUSK when Benjamin slammed out of the house automatically walking toward the graveyard to talk to Anna. He knelt at her grave, brushing the leaves away. In the time since he'd been there the leaves had gone from pretty oranges and reds to a dull brown. They littered the ground on top of her grave.

"I'm confused, Anna. I thought Emily was such a good woman. She's been a real blessing to the girls and to me, but

Mor told me she said some horrible things to her. The person I thought she was would never have been so rude to my mother." He sighed heavily. "What if I'm doing the wrong thing by leaving her alone with our girls all day every day?

"And what's more, when I was talking to *Far* today, I realized that I love her. I still love you, of course. You'll always hold a huge place in my heart, but there's some room left for another good woman. I thought Emily was the woman I needed to complete my life and that of the girls. I don't know what I was thinking. How could I have lost my heart to a woman who would disrespect *Mor*?

"I'm so confused. I want what's best for the girls, of course, and Emily seems to be doing a good job with them." He grinned. "You should see the way the girls jump up after every meal to clear the table and do the dishes. Georgie has to stand on a chair, but she does it, and she dries them beautifully. You'd be so proud of our girls. And the dresses she made them. I swear they look more like you every day." He traced his finger over her name. "But how can the woman who has done such nice things for my girls, and who cooks meals better than anyone I've ever met be the same woman *Mor* cried to me about today?

"I just left. It was our first real argument. I slammed the door and left. I feel like she's betrayed me, but deep down, I don't know what I'd do without her. She didn't fill your shoes, because no one could have, but she completed our lives in a way I thought would never happen. I guess I should apologize, but I don't think I've done anything wrong."

He stood up looking down at the grave in the darkness that had settled over the town. "I wish I could hear your answers, because you always knew the right thing to say. I miss you, Anna."

He turned back toward the house, walking slowly, not in any hurry to see his wife again.

When he went inside, he found her setting the table. She'd made a quick meal of fried potatoes with bacon and the leftover corn chowder. The girls were pouring milk into their glasses.

Once they were sitting, he looked at Emily, and saw her eyes were red rimmed as if she'd been crying. His heart hurt knowing he'd made her cry, but she'd made his *mor* cry. He couldn't let her get away with treating people badly. He wasn't sure how things were done back East, but here everyone respected their elders.

He bowed his head and said a quick prayer over the meal. The girls kept looking back and forth between the two of them as if they knew something was wrong, but they weren't sure what.

After dinner, he went to the parlor, while she went upstairs to get the laundry gathered up for the morning. While she read a chapter of *Little Women* to the girls, he sat in the parlor waiting for her to come back down to talk to him. Finally, long after they usually went to bed, he went upstairs to check on her and saw the light was out when he looked under the door. He opened it to find she wasn't there. Where was she?

He opened the door to Georgie's room, and Georgie was sound asleep, so he closed it again quietly. He peeked into Abbie's room, and there she was. She'd fallen asleep on Abbie's bed with her, the book still open on the bed in front of her. He turned down the lamp and left her there, not willing to wake either of them. They'd talk in the morning.

CHAPTER 9

*E*mily was decidedly cold toward Benjamin the following morning. His breakfast was warm and waiting when he got up and she was cordial, but there was none of the playfulness in her eyes. Benjamin hadn't realized how much he'd come to look forward to his wife's smiles.

As the days wore on, he could see she hadn't forgiven him for taking his *Mor's* side in their tiff. How could she honestly expect him to believe a woman he had just met over his own mother? How could any woman expect that?

She helped in the store when he asked her to, and she made dresses for herself and the girls. Her food continued to be so good it made his mouth water, but she never asked if he was in the mood for her to cook anything special like she did with the girls. He missed her kind smiles.

Emily never turned him away during the night, but the sadness in her eyes, often kept him from starting anything with her. Her eyes reminded him of a lost puppy who couldn't figure out why no one loved it like they should. He wanted to apologize, but he couldn't choose her over his own mother. What kind of person would that make him?

Every day he felt her growing more and more distant, wondering what he could do to stop it, but knowing there was only one answer. He'd have to agree that she must be telling the truth about *Mor*, and that he could never do.

Several weeks after his argument with Emily, his *mor* invited them out to the farm for a family dinner after church. He thought it would be a perfect opportunity for Emily and his mother to work things out, so he readily agreed. As they walked home from church, he told Emily they were going to go out to the farm for lunch, and she stopped in her tracks.

"Benjamin Johnson, you're mad if you think I'm going to go out to that house and let your mother treat me like I'm not good enough to be in your life again. I'm an adult, and I have the right to choose who I will and will not be around. I choose not to be around her." She crossed her arms over her chest and glared at him. It was snowing and the flakes clung to her lashes, making her look particularly pretty to him.

"This will give you and *Mor* a chance to talk and make things right between you." His eyes were pleading with her not to argue with him. He wanted to see the end of her animosity toward his mother. He couldn't stand much more anger in his household.

"Did your mother say she wanted to make things right? Or are you assuming she wants to?"

He looked down, and she had her answer. Her mother-in-law had no desire to make things right with her, because she saw her as a temporary guest in her son's household. For a woman who professed to be Christian, she was certainly willing for her son to divorce.

"Please, Emily. I don't want there to be any more hard feelings between us." His voice was pleading with her, and she almost felt guilty for what she knew her answer had to be.

She shook her head adamantly. "There wouldn't be hard

feelings between us if she would start treating me like a person instead of a piece of cow dung on her favorite church shoe." She realized the girls were listening to the argument. "You girls run on ahead. We'll be there in a minute." She smiled as she spoke to the girls to try and soften what they'd heard her say to their father.

"I want our marriage to work, Emily. I care for you a great deal, and I think you make a wonderful mother for the girls. Would you please try?"

She noticed he'd said he cared for her. Not he loved her. She shook her head. "There's no reason for me to try. Your mother has made it clear she doesn't want me in her house. I won't go back." She shrugged. "You're welcome to go by yourself or take the girls. I can stay home alone. It won't hurt me one bit." She started walking toward the house without another word. She'd never been stubborn about anything in her life, but this was something she would not back down on. She couldn't let him take his mother's side over hers and still hold her head up. She simply couldn't.

"I can't go without you. What would I tell *Mor*?"

"I really don't care what you tell your mother. Did you care how I'd feel about going to her house with the way she treats me?" She didn't pause as she hurried to the house. Once she was inside, she went into the kitchen and started a fire in the stove in the kitchen.

Benjamin sighed as he watched her walk away. How was he ever going to make things right with his wife again?

~

BENJAMIN WENT into the barn to talk to *Far* while Georgie stayed in the house to play with his *mor*. Abbie had adamantly refused to leave saying she wanted to stay with Emily. He threw his arms up and left them both, Georgie happily skipping along behind him. The little girl seemed oblivious to the fight he'd just had with Emily, even though she'd witnessed most of it.

"I don't know what to do." He knew his voice was defeated as he went to the one man in the world who always had the right words to help him.

Far looked up at him from where he was leaning against the stall of one of the horses. "About Emily refusing to come out to see us?"

Benjamin had made up an excuse about Abbie having a tummy ache and needing to stay home and Emily staying to nurse her. His mother's eyes had narrowed at the words, but *Far* had just nodded as if he'd expected it. "You knew I was lying?" He'd been worried about that. He hadn't wanted to lie to them, but how could he tell his parents his wife refused to go into his mother's home?

"Yah. And so did your *mor*."

"I hated lying to you, but Emily's made up some story about how *Mor* tells her she's not good enough to be my wife and not good enough to be the mother of my children. She says *Mor* says hateful things the moment my back is turned." Benjamin kicked at the hay on the floor of the barn. "I thought she was such a sweet woman, but she really seems to hate *Mor*." He hated admitting he'd made such a huge mistake to his father.

Far watched Benjamin for a moment. "What makes you think Emily made the story up?"

Benjamin stared at his father for a moment before he realized he must be joking. "Well, of course she made it up. *Mor* wouldn't treat anyone that way. Especially not someone who made the girls and me so happy." He sighed, knowing his father wouldn't like someone who could treat his wife so badly.

"You were our youngest, so you probably didn't notice a

lot of things that happened under our roof over the years. Your *mor* is one of the most headstrong women I've ever met." Sven removed his pipe from his pocket and lit it. "I love her, but she's not the perfect woman you have in your head."

Benjamin shook his head. "*Mor* wouldn't do the things Emily says she does. There's no way. She loves the girls and me too much to try to cause animosity between my wife and me. And Emily admitted to me she'd told *Mor* she didn't respect her. What kind of woman would say that to her mother-in-law?" How could *Far* try to defend Emily after what he'd just told him? What was wrong with him?

Sven shrugged. "You'll believe what you want to believe. Just remember, good women are hard to find. You've found two of them to love in your short life. Don't do anything to push her away."

Benjamin thought about his father's words during the drive back to town. Georgie sat beside him jabbering on about her day happy she was able to be the center of attention on the way home with no worry about interruption. She'd apparently had a wonderful day with her grandmother. The *Mor* he knew loved him and her granddaughters with everything inside her. She just couldn't do what Emily had accused her of. No matter what *Far* said.

~

EMILY HAD ENJOYED her day home alone with Abbie immensely. They'd spent some time reading together and Emily had worked on showing Abbie the days of the week and the months on the calendar, trying to teach her more things she'd need to learn before school started in September.

It was while Emily was teaching Abbie about the months of the year that she realized she had missed her monthly cycle. It was the beginning of October the last time she'd had it. She looked carefully at the calendar realizing it was now the beginning of December. She'd already started making the Christmas gifts for the girls. She counted the days on the calendar one more time, trying not to alarm Abbie as she stared at the calendar.

"What are you looking at, Mama?"

Emily smiled. "Do you realize I've been here for six weeks now? I can't believe I've been blessed to be your mother for that long."

Abbie moved over next to Emily and hugged her tightly. "I'm so glad you're here. I've never known anyone who was so much like me before."

"You mean, because I'm shy and don't like being around big crowds either?" Emily stroked Abbie's hair out of her face as she asked the question. Abbie's hair was always coming out of her braids and hanging loose around her face.

Abbie nodded. "I like to be at home and so do you."

"I do. It's nice to have a daughter who's just like me." Emily wondered about the child she was obviously carrying. How could she not have realized before? She should have known a month ago she was expecting. Would her new child be more like Abbie or Georgie? Or somewhere in between? Would it be a boy or a girl? She liked the idea of having a son, just because she didn't have one, but she loved the girls so much, she knew she'd be thrilled with another.

And how could she tell Benjamin? They were barely on speaking terms. Did he even have a right to know? Could she raise a child with a man who didn't respect her enough to believe her when she told him about a problem she had? It wasn't like she went to Benjamin with problems every day. She'd gone to him with one serious problem, and he'd all but called her a liar. No, there was no way she could raise a child with him.

She thought about what Harriett Long had said in the

train station. If she wasn't respected and treated well by her husband then she shouldn't stay. Should she write Harriett and ask for a train ticket home? And if she did, where would she stay? Harriett had promised to help her if she found herself in a bad situation, but Benjamin didn't mistreat her exactly. He'd never hit her at least.

"Mama! Mama!"

Emily shook her head. She'd been so lost in thought she hadn't noticed Abbie saying something to her. "I'm sorry, Abbie, what is it?"

"I asked if we could bake cookies now. You said we could make some for Georgie and Papa when they came home."

"Of course we can!" Emily got to her feet and walked to the work table in the kitchen getting down the ingredients. She took the recipe she'd carefully written out for Abbie out of the pocket of her apron and smoothed it onto the table. She had promised Abbie that this time, she'd just watch to keep her from making mistakes, but Abbie could bake the cookies all on her own.

~

BENJAMIN WALKED into the house and smelled the cookies baking in the oven. He was so happy Emily wasn't mad at his girls, or he was certain he wouldn't be receiving sweets every day. He walked into the kitchen to see Abbie carefully removing a pan of cookies from the oven while Emily watched over her.

He wanted to warn her the pan was hot, but the way Emily was hovering, he knew she'd heard the warning multiple times. She turned to Emily and smiled. "I did it. They smell good!"

Georgie bounced into the kitchen. "Cookies! Yummy!"

Abbie turned to her sister. "They have to cool for a few

minutes, but then we can try them. Mama let me make them all by myself!"

"I want to make cookies all by myself!" Georgie turned to Emily. "When can I make cookies by myself?"

Emily smiled down at her younger daughter. "When you're six. You have to be big enough to get the cookies in and out of the oven to really do it by yourself."

She turned to Abbie. "Why don't you go sit down, and I'll pour milk for everyone? Since you did the cooking, I'll serve."

Abbie sat down looking so proud of herself it made Benjamin's chest hurt. Always before she'd been shunted to the side because Georgie demanded so much attention. It was good to see his elder daughter proud of something she'd done for a change. Emily had worked a miracle with the girl, and deserved to be praised for it.

Georgie and Benjamin sat at the table beside Abbie while Emily took plates down off the shelf and poured them each a glass of milk. She put two cookies on each plate and sat down across from Abbie. "You need to take the first bite, Abbie," Emily urged. "You made them!"

Benjamin looked down at the perfectly shaped cookie. He knew his daughter had worked hard to make them and felt an overwhelming sense of pride in her. How could he not have realized how much Abbie needed to be treated like she was special to really shine?

Abbie bit into her cookie and smiled. "It tastes just like yours, Mama!"

Benjamin bit into his own cookie. "This is delicious. This doesn't taste just like your mama's, though." When Abbie's face fell, he smiled at her, and took another bite. "It's better!"

Abbie turned red with embarrassment. "Thank you, Papa."

Emily's eyes caught Benjamin's across the table and she

smiled, nodding slightly letting him know she was glad he'd praised Abbie.

Once they were done with their cookies, Emily insisted Abbie go into the parlor with Benjamin while she and Georgie cleared the table and washed the few dishes. "The cook shouldn't have to clean," Emily told them.

~

THE FOLLOWING AFTERNOON, Emily rang up customers for an hour while Benjamin worked in the backroom doing inventory. He'd found he enjoyed having a bit of time to himself in the afternoons, and it was good for Emily to meet more people in the community. The girls were upstairs playing quietly while they waited for Emily to come back so they could all make supper together.

He heard the bell over the door tinkle signaling a customer, but knew Emily could handle things, so he went back to counting. He heard his *mor's* voice and that of her friend, Clara. Clara was Kristen's mother, and he knew she was miffed he'd married someone other than her daughter. He thought about going out to let Emily slip away without having to talk to her, but decided it was time she made things right with his mother.

"I can't believe Benjamin lets you run the store during the day," Ingrid began. "You don't know the first thing about being a mother or a wife, and that's what you're here for. How could he possibly think you could handle the store? Make sure you don't take money from the cash register." Ingrid was silent for a moment. "Of course, if she'd take it and buy herself a train ticket back East where she belongs, I wouldn't complain."

Clara laughed. "I've heard you can't even cook simple

Norwegian foods. What was Benjamin thinking marrying you?"

"She's trying to turn my granddaughters against me, too! Why, just yesterday she refused to come out to my house when I extended an invitation for Sunday dinner. You'd think she'd be happy to come out and learn to cook properly, but she didn't bother to come. My poor son had to come out and make excuses for her. She even kept Abbie here in town and wouldn't let her come see me."

"Good afternoon, Mrs. Johnson. Mrs. Olafsen. Is there something I can help you find today?" Emily's sweet voice sounded calm as she asked the question as if she hadn't even heard the way the two older women had insulted her. "We've just received a new shipment of calico. Would you like to see it?"

"You're not fooling anyone with your sweet act, Emily. My son sees you for what you are finally. I've never seen him as unhappy as he was yesterday." *Mor's* voice was filled with happiness as she talked about how unhappy he was. What was going on?

"Does this mean you don't want to see the new shipment of calico?" Emily asked.

Benjamin couldn't help but grin. His wife was holding her own against the two old biddies. How could his mother try to split up his marriage that way? Why would she do such a thing? Emily was the best thing that had happened to his family in a long time. Why didn't his mother see that?

"Of course, we don't want to see the calico! All we want to see is your backside when you're on your way out of town!" *Mor's* voice was downright vindictive as she said the words.

Benjamin carefully laid down his inventory papers and walked around the shelf that separated the back room from the main store. He arrived just in time to see his mother deliberately knock over a display of ribbons. "Oops. I suppose you'll have to pick those up."

Who was this woman with the eyes flashing with hate? How could his mother treat a sweet woman like Emily the way she was? He knew without a doubt his mother had been the one lying. He wanted to drop to his knees right then and beg Emily's forgiveness, but he knew he needed to let his mother know what he thought of her first.

"*Mor?*"

As soon as she heard his voice, Ingrid paled. "Benjamin? How long have you been standing there?"

"Long enough to see you deliberately knock over a display in my store to cause my wife more work." He didn't add he'd been listening from the back room to everything she'd said since she came into the store.

"Oh, Benjamin. She told me I wasn't welcome in the store any longer, and she wanted me to stay away from my granddaughters. I was upset, and I wasn't thinking. I'll pick them up." She knelt down and began picking up all the ribbons she'd knocked to the floor.

"So you were only upset because Emily was mean to you again?" he asked, acting as if he believed every word she had said.

Emily's face was red, but she didn't say anything to defend herself. He knew she didn't think he'd believe her, and who could blame her? He'd done nothing but call her a liar for weeks. He didn't deserve to have a woman as good as Emily in his life. He only hoped he could get her to stay for the girls.

His *mor* stood up and met his eyes. "That's exactly it. I don't know why she hates me so much." A tear trickled out of the corner of her eye for effect.

He wondered then why his mother hadn't made her living on the stage. *Far* had been right. His mother wasn't anything like what he'd thought she was. He walked across the room toward his mother with a concerned look on his face. Once he was close, he leaned down and whispered, "Have you always been a vindictive liar, *Mor*, or is this something new?"

His mother backed up a step as if to get away from him. She'd never seen anything but adoration in his eyes. Her other children had seen her for what she was years before, which was why she seldom had a houseful of family on Sundays after church, and why she depended on Benjamin coming out so often. "What do you mean?"

Benjamin reached out and removed the spool of ribbon from her hands before gripping her shoulders and turning her toward the door. As he pushed her out the door of his store, he told her, "I've been fortunate enough to be loved by two women in my life. Both have been wonderful, but I have to say, I never thought I'd find someone like Emily. She's taken in my daughters as if they were her own. She cooks for us, cleans for us, and does everything she can to make us comfortable and happy. I'd think you'd be thrilled that she came into our lives. Instead, you spend your time trying to find a way to get her to leave me. You treat her like she's not good enough to be a part of our family. Why? Why would you do that?"

Mor turned around and glared at him. "She's not even Norwegian. She can't cook for you! How can she cook your favorite foods and teach the girls to cook good Norwegian meals when she doesn't know how?"

He blinked a few times. "You've done all this because my wife doesn't know how to cook Norwegian foods? Let me tell you something. I'd rather eat what my wife cooks any day of the week than eat your fine Norwegian cooking. She may not cook Norwegian, but she's a far better cook than you are, because she cooks with something you seem to be missing inside you. She cooks, and does everything in her life with love." He opened the door, and pushed her through it. "Go away, *Mor*. You can come back when you're ready to apologize to my wife and treat her like the wonderful woman she is. As far as I'm concerned, you're no longer my *mor*, and my daughters are no longer your granddaughters. Tell *Far* he's welcome to see them as long as you're not with them." He slammed the shop door in her face, while a shocked Clara Olafsen and Emily looked on.

He ignored Clara and walked across the shop to Emily, dropping to his knees at her feet. "Emily, my sweet wonderful wife, will you forgive me for being an idiot and believing my *mor*, when I should have believed you?"

Emily covered her mouth with her hand to stifle the giggle that was threatening to come out and nodded.

Benjamin got to his feet and pulled her into his arms, kissing her right there in the middle of the store when anyone could walk in right in front of Clara. "I don't deserve your forgiveness, but I will happily take it. You're the best thing that could have possibly happened to my girls and me."

She sighed and snuggled into his arms, not caring if it was the proper thing to do for a change. "I love you, Benjamin," she whispered.

He pulled away looking down into her face to try to read her eyes to see if she was telling the truth. "I'm so glad, because I love you."

He kissed her one last time before sighing. "It's too early to close up shop, but you need to get back upstairs to our girls." He pushed her toward the back room. "I'll be up as soon as I can."

She smiled, looking forward to it. Maybe they could make their marriage work after all.

CHAPTER 10

*B*enjamin hurried up to the house after work that evening. He found Emily in the kitchen as usual, finishing up supper. The table was set, but the girls were nowhere to be seen. He stepped up behind Emily and wrapped his arms around her kissing the side of her neck while she stirred the stew on the stove.

"Supper's almost ready," she told him as she tilted her head to the side to give him better access.

"I feel terrible about not believing you."

She turned in his arms. "You should." Her eyes met his, but he could see the hurt that was still there. "I appreciate the fact that you finally figured out your mother was lying to you, but it still hurts that you didn't believe me from the beginning. I've never lied to you, yet you immediately jumped to the conclusion that I must be lying."

He shook his head. "I honestly have been afraid of falling in love with you since you got here. How I felt had just hit me while I was talking with *Far* when *Mor* told me those lies about you. Anna and *Mor* loved each other. Anna was another daughter to her, probably because we'd grown up together." He stroked his hands over her shoulders soothingly as he spoke. "I'd been praising you and talking about what an amazing woman you are when we stepped outside and I saw you waiting beside the buggy for me instead of staying in the house and helping *Mor*. I have no excuse other than believing what *Mor* said made it easier to decide I couldn't know everything there was to know about you, so I must not be in love."

"But why wouldn't you want to love me? Was I so repulsive to you?" Her voice was filled with hurt, but her eyes met his straight on.

"Of course not!" He turned away pacing across the kitchen as he tried to find the best way to explain how he felt. "I've known Anna since our first day of school. We played together at recess, and I played all the usual pranks on her. She was a part of my life for twenty years. I think I knew I would marry her from the time I was twelve years old." He swallowed hard before continuing. "Just sending off for a mail order bride made me feel as if I was betraying Anna. The girls needed a mother so badly, but I felt like I should wait another year or two. But I didn't. I gave in to their needs, because I love them. I expected to see you as a friend, and maybe a partner in parenting, that I had the added benefit of sharing a bed with."

She sighed and turned away from him, checking on the biscuits in the oven.

"I really didn't want to love you, but I couldn't help myself. You were so good with the girls from the first day. Anna was a good mother to both girls, but she could never understand Abbie. They simply didn't mesh well." He frowned. "I'm not criticizing Anna, but she wasn't the mother Abbie needed. Abbie was way too quiet for Anna to be able to understand her. She was so much like Georgie."

Emily didn't comment as she took the biscuits out of the

oven and carefully put them on a plate for the table. Her feelings were hurt, but she tried not to show it. How could she explain her hurt over the fact that he didn't want to love her? Did it even make any sense?

"I couldn't have found a better mother for my girls if I'd interviewed a thousand women." He put his hand on her arm to stop her from putting the biscuits on the table. "Emily, you've completed my family. You are what I need in life and I love you more than I ever dreamed possible."

Emily looked up at him with tears streaming down her face. "But you didn't want to love me? Why wouldn't you want to love me? What's wrong with me?"

He sighed, hating himself for making her cry, and looking for the right words to explain how he'd been feeling without making matters worse. "There's nothing wrong with you. I just felt like falling for my new wife would be a betrayal of Anna." He wiped one of Emily's tears from her cheek with his thumb. "I love you, and if that's a betrayal, I'm sorry, but it doesn't change anything. I need you in my life."

She nodded for a moment, still unsure if he was telling her the truth or what he thought she wanted to hear. "I love you, too. I never knew Anna, but she sounds like she was a good wife to you. I don't want to take her place, you know. I just want to be the best wife and mother I can be. Whether I do it like Anna did or not."

He pulled her to him stroking her back as he just held her. "It's time for me to move on with my life. The girls already have, and I'm moving on as well." He kissed the top of her head. "Who knows? Maybe we'll have children of our own someday."

Emily bit her lip, knowing she needed to tell him her news. She leaned back and looked up at his face. "There's something I need to tell you." Would he be happy with the news? Their love was so new to both of them. Would adding a child into the mix help things or just hurt them?

He brushed a kiss across her forehead. "What do you want to tell me?"

"That child of our own you mentioned?"

"Uh huh?"

"It's going to be here sooner than you realized. I'm thinking around eight months from now." Emily watched Benjamin's face carefully for his reaction. Would he be pleased?

His face lit up with a huge grin. "Are you sure?"

She nodded. "I haven't seen a doctor, but I'm sure." Her eyes searched his. "Are you happy?"

He held her close. "How could I not be happy? I love children. I'd be thrilled to have another dozen."

"Mama! I'm starving!" They looked over to see Georgie standing just inside the kitchen. "You said we'd be eating in a few minutes and that was hours and hours ago."

Emily laughed and pulled away from Benjamin. "It's only been a few minutes, but it is time to eat. Go get your sister and wash up." Trust Georgie to be the one to ruin an important moment.

Georgie ran off to get Abbie.

"Do you want a boy or a girl?" Benjamin asked.

Emily shrugged. "We have two girls, so a boy would be nice, but I would love to have more girls too. I'd like to have some of each, but I don't really care which comes first."

"Do you mind if we tell the girls at dinner?" he asked.

"Not at all. I think they'll be thrilled. Abbie's been making noise about wanting more brothers and sisters already anyway." Emily put the butter on the table as she talked. "I think we're going to have two very excited little girls on our hands."

After Benjamin said the prayer for them, he told the girls, "Emily and I have something to tell you."

141

Abbie looked up at Emily with fear in her eyes. "You're not leaving are you? You can't leave us, Mama! We need you!" She stood and ran from the table.

Emily stood, shaking her head at Benjamin to indicate he needed to stay where he was. "You and Georgie eat. I'll go talk to her."

She hurried out of the kitchen and up to Abbie's room. Knocking softly on the door, she called, "It's just me, Abbie. May I come in?" She could hear Abbie crying through the door.

"No, go away! I know you don't want to be here anyway!"

Emily pushed the door open and went to sit on the side of Abbie's bed. "Of course, I want to be here. This family is the most important thing in the world to me. I'm never leaving."

Abbie kept her face buried in her pillow. "But *Farmor* said...."

Emily sighed. Her mother-in-law had said altogether too much lately. She stroked her hand over Abbie's hair. "What did she say?"

Abbie sat up sniffling. "She said you didn't love us, and you belong out East. She said you weren't meant to be our mother or you'd have been born Norwegian." She ran her hand under her nose, wiping it on her sleeve. "I don't care if you're Norwegian or not. I just want you to stay and keep being my mama."

"I'm not going anywhere, Abbie. I promise."

"What was Papa going to tell us then?"

Emily stood and held her hand out for Abbie. "Why don't we go find out? I'm sure he waited for us, because he wanted to tell you and Georgie together."

They walked back down to the table hand in hand. Emily was happy that Abbie wanted her as a mother so badly, but she wished she could convince the girl that she loved her and would never leave.

Emily smiled and nodded at Benjamin to let him know everything was okay as she sat down with Abbie at her side.

Abbie looked at her father, her eyes still bright with tears. "What were you going to tell us, Papa?"

Benjamin glanced between Emily and Abbie, but knew he'd have to wait until later for answers. "You're going to have a little brother or sister."

Abbie's eyes widened as she turned and stared at Emily. "A baby? You're really going to have a baby?" When Emily smiled and nodded, she launched herself out of her chair on top of her mother. "That means you're really not leaving! Oh, Mama! I'm so happy you're going to stay with us forever!"

Emily hugged Abbie while stroking her hair. "I keep telling you I'm not going anywhere."

Abbie buried her face in Emily's neck and didn't say a word, just content to be there.

Benjamin looked at Georgie. "So are you happy to be getting a new brother or sister?"

Georgie shrugged. "Sounds good to me. I want someone to boss around like Abbie bosses me around." She grinned at Emily. "Can I help with the baby?"

Emily smiled. "I'm going to need lots and lots of help with the baby. I won't be able to do it without you girls."

Abbie pulled away from Emily, her face streaked with tears. "I love you, Mama," she whispered.

Emily stroked Abbie's cheek. "I love you too, and I'm never going anywhere. I'm happy here."

Abbie sniffled one last time before settling into her chair to finally eat her dinner.

Emily's eyes met Benjamin's across the table and he reached out and took her hand while saying, "Our family is going to be fine."

Emily and Abbie were just putting dessert on the table when they heard a commotion coming from downstairs.

Benjamin went to investigate while Emily cut the apple pie she and Abbie had spent the morning making. Abbie poured fresh milk for them all and they resumed their seats waiting for Benjamin to return before eating the pie.

Benjamin came in, his eyes on Emily, trying to help her remain calm. Behind him were his parents, his father dragging his mother behind him.

Benjamin took his seat at the table, still watching Emily, worried how she'd react to his *mor* being in her home after the way she'd treated her.

Emily stood up. "Would you like some pie? Abbie and I made it just this morning." Her eyes were on her father in law, but the offer was for both of them.

Sven pushed Ingrid in front of him toward Emily, obviously forcing her to say something.

Ingrid looked over her shoulder at Sven before clearing her throat. "I'm sorry, Emily. I've been nothing but rude to you since you came here. You've been a good mother to my girls and a good wife to Benjamin. I should be thanking you for being a good mother to the girls, but instead I try to make you go back to the East."

Emily nodded. She'd expected an apology, because she knew her mother-in-law wanted to be able to keep in contact with her son and granddaughters. She knew she couldn't possibly mean it, though. Her mother-in-law still considered her inferior in every way. There was no doubt in Emily's mind the apology was coerced and meant nothing. She was at least acknowledging her bad behavior, though, and Emily wasn't going to be rude. "I love your son and granddaughters. I'll do whatever I can to make them comfortable." She paused as she put two more pieces of pie on plates for her in laws, although they hadn't said whether they wanted them yet. "I'm not going back East, no matter what happens. Marriage is forever, and I belong here with my family."

Sven took the pie offered him and sat down to fork up a bite. Ingrid stood looking down at the pie for a moment before taking a seat as well. "I won't do anything else to try to make you leave. I promise."

"Thank you for that." Emily resumed her seat next to Abbie.

"I should have offered a long time ago to offer to teach you to cook Norwegian foods. My son and granddaughters have the right to eat their favorite foods in their own home."

Before Emily could answer, Benjamin said, "Emily is the best cook I've ever known. I like what she cooks better than the Norwegian foods I grew up eating. She doesn't need to learn to cook Norwegian to keep my family happy."

Emily stared in shock at Benjamin. She'd never heard him say anything even remotely rude to his mother before today, and she was trying to apologize, and he was still being rude. "I'd still like to learn to prepare your favorite dishes."

He shrugged. "I haven't missed them, and I'll still eat them when we go to *Mor's*. I don't need to have Norwegian cooking at home." His eyes met his mother's as he said the words, letting her know just how strong his backing of Emily was.

Ingrid took a bite of the apple pie in front of her, at a loss as to why her son was behaving the way he was. Her eyes widened. "This is very good. Maybe I should be coming to you for cooking lessons." Ingrid had been very proud of her cooking. For years, she'd been the undisputed best cook in the area with requests for her pies for weddings frequent.

Emily hid her smile. "I enjoy your cooking."

Abbie smiled her whole face lighting up as she watched her grandmother finally being nice to her new mama. "My mama is the best cook in the whole wide world."

Sven smiled at Abbie. "You may just be right about that, Abbie."

Georgie looked at Ingrid. "*Farmor*, we're having a baby!"

Ingrid's hand went to her throat in surprise. "A baby?" She looked at Benjamin who gave a quick nod. "Another grandchild? And I've been causing you stress?" She jumped up from her chair and began clearing the table. "If there's anything you need to help you, just let me know. I can start coming into town a couple days per week to help with the housework."

Emily laughed. "I'm pregnant, not an invalid. I'm perfectly capable of taking care of my family."

"Have you been sick in the mornings?"

"Just a little, but I'm sure it's coming."

"When I got to the worst of my morning sickness, I'd always bake up muffins the night before and let everyone have cold muffins in the mornings. I had a hard time even thinking about cooking my stomach was so upset."

Emily nodded. "That's how it was for my employer in Massachusetts as well. She couldn't even come into the room when I cooked breakfast. Most of the time I'd take her some dry toast and some tea." Emily got to her feet and worked side by side with her mother-in-law doing the dishes and cleaning up.

Georgie and Abbie helped them with the clearing, and then Abbie swept out from under the table. Ingrid looked over her shoulders and watched the girls work. "You've got the girls working so much harder than I've ever seen them. They always complained when Anna or I told them to work. What's your secret?"

Emily shrugged. "I've just always asked nicely and shown them how to do it properly. They both seem to like being useful." She quickly dried the dishes as her mother-in-law washed them. Within minutes they were finished and the girls were sitting at the table with the men.

Ingrid hugged Emily tightly. "I'm really sorry for never giving you a chance. I promise to do better." She looked over at Sven sitting at the table talking to Benjamin. "Let's go! I need to get home and start making a quilt for my new grandbaby." Ingrid shrugged into her coat and wrapped her scarf around her head as Sven got to his feet. "I know just the colors I want to use." She looked at Benjamin. "You're going to need to add onto this house. It's not going to be nearly big enough if she has babies this quickly." Ingrid was practically bouncing up and down at the idea of lots more grandchildren. "I'll never have enough grandbabies!" She hurried down the stairs with her husband watching after her.

Sven went to follow but turned to Emily at the last minute. "We're thankful you're the one who married Benjamin. We couldn't ask for a better daughter in law." He didn't wait for her reply, but headed down the stairs after his wife.

Emily turned to Benjamin with a surprised look on her face. He grinned. "That's the mama I know and love. I really am sorry I didn't believe you when you said how she was treating you. It just didn't make sense to me."

They went into the parlor to spend a quiet evening. Emily worked on sewing a dress for Abbie, while Benjamin read the paper. Abbie and Georgie sat in the corner on the floor playing with their baby dolls. Emily noted the frayed condition of the dolls' clothes and promised herself she'd make them new doll clothes for Christmas. They could use a couple of doll quilts as well. She smiled as she thought of the looks on their faces when they opened them.

She couldn't help but look forward to next Christmas when there would be another child to make gifts for. How had she been so blessed? Just months before when her mother had told her she had two months to find a new home, she'd never imagined her life could take such a turn. She needed to write to her mother and let her know how happy she was.

In bed that night, she snuggled close against Benjamin's side after making love. He'd been gentler than ever, obviously thinking about the baby growing inside her. "Are you happy about the baby?" he asked in a low tone.

She lifted her head from his shoulder to look down at him in the darkness. "How can you even ask that? Of course, I'm happy about the baby. I can think of nothing that would make me happier!"

"Are you sure?" Benjamin's voice was worried.

"I'm positive. I love children. I can't wait to hold one in my arms."

"You're so young. I hate that you're giving up your freedom to be tied down with a baby."

She laughed. "You had Abbie at my age."

"But I'd had years of courtship and loving my wife. You're just starting a new marriage, and already you're having a baby. We had two years with no children before Anna got pregnant." He stroked her cheek as she lay propped above him on the bed.

"We started this marriage with children, and I wouldn't trade that for anything. I knew I was going to be an instant mother when I married you, and I'm happy I was. I love the girls and I love you. I'm very happy to be having a baby. I've always wanted one. I wish I hadn't missed those early years with the girls, but I can't go back and change that now."

He pulled her back down so her head was pillowed on his shoulder. "I'm glad. When you told me about the baby, all I could think about was how happy I was and how glad the girls would be. I never thought to wonder how it would make you feel to have another child."

She rubbed her cheek against his smooth shoulder.

"There was no need to wonder how I'd feel about it. I'm thrilled. I can't wait to see its little face."

He held her close in the darkness. "I do love you, Emily. I'm sorry that I made you feel bad."

She shook her head. "I'm fine. I guess I just feel like I'm constantly in competition with Anna, which is silly, but I can't get it out of my head that you chose her, but you found me by chance."

"Never feel like you're less than Anna. In some ways, you're a much better wife and mother. For our first year of marriage, she couldn't cook anything without burning it, and she'd cry if I didn't eat all of it."

Emily grinned. "Well, I certainly don't do that!"

"No, you're a great cook. Georgie hasn't had to eat one bacon sandwich since you got here." He smiled thinking about the letter they'd sent that had brought her to them. "You're a more natural mother than Anna was, too. Anna was unsure of everything. She loved the girls, but she was constantly running to her mother or mine when anything went a little bit wrong. She'd have had no idea how to handle Abbie this evening, but you acted as if it was something you've dealt with every day."

"I think Abbie is so easy for me because she's just so much like I was. I don't know what to do with Georgie except love her. I'm good at loving her."

He chuckled and her head shook on his shoulder. "No worries. Your love will get us all through." He stroked his fingers through her hair. "I wonder if the baby will be a boy or a girl. I love my girls, but the idea of having a boy really excites me. Of course, I wouldn't know what to do with a boy after having two girls."

She smiled stroking his chest. "We'll figure it out together if it happens. I'd be thrilled either way. Just so I have a baby in my arms, I'll be happy."

EPILOGUE

 ne year later

"Hurry and finish dressing girls. They'll be here any minute!" Emily had waited until the last minute before having the girls change from their play clothes.

She checked on baby Clarence in his cradle before she made the last minute preparations. There was hot coffee on the stove, and a batch of freshly baked cookies cooling on the work table. She had a huge pot of stew on the stove in case they were hungry when they arrived.

She couldn't believe they were finally coming out to see her and meet her family. She heard the door open and flew down the stairs flinging herself into her mother's arms. "Mama! You really made it!"

"I promised I'd be here, and I'm here!" Jane pulled back from her daughter. "Where are my grandchildren?"

Emily smiled and swiped the tears from her eyes before sliding her hand through her mother's arm and walking up the steps with her. "The girls are changing into clean clothes and Clarence is asleep."

Abbie and Georgie were waiting for them in the kitchen. They'd changed into clean dresses and Abbie had brushed her sister's hair until it hung in an untangled heap down her back. Abbie's own hair was still in the two braids Emily had put it into that morning. "These are my girls, Mama. The older one is Abbie, and the younger is Georgie."

Georgie barreled across the kitchen to hug her new grandmother, not at all worried about her reception. Abbie held back, but soon followed and hugged Jane as well.

Abbie had become more confident in the year Emily had been with them, but her personality was still as quiet and shy as ever. Georgie was as boisterous as she had always been.

Jane smiled at the two girls. "It's hard to believe I have granddaughters who are half grown already." She turned to Emily. "I know you said Clarence is sleeping, but can we peek in on him?"

Emily led the way into the parlor where a cradle was kept for Clarence's naps. Jane put her hand over her mouth as the tears filled her eyes at the sight of her grandson. He was sleeping on his stomach with his fist firmly in his mouth. "He's beautiful, Emily."

Emily nodded. "He's as blond as everyone else. I'm going to have to keep having babies until I have one with dark hair."

Jane laughed. "I'll take as many grandbabies as you want to give me."

"Let's go have some cookies in the kitchen. I made a big pot of coffee to go with them."

"That sounds heavenly."

Benjamin came up the stairs with William at his side. Emily smiled at her stepfather. "It's good to see you, William."

"You have a beautiful home."

"Thank you." Emily was unsure what to say to him. She didn't harbor any bad feelings toward him, because her life had turned out so well and she was truly happy. "Have a seat. I made coffee and the girls helped me bake some cookies."

Benjamin had made the long drive into St. Paul that morning to pick the couple up from the train station there. Emily had never really expected to see her mother again, so she was thrilled they were able to make the long journey.

Clarence began to wail from the other room, and her mother jumped up. "May I get him?"

"Of course!" Emily continued pouring out the coffee and readying the snack she'd prepared.

Within a minute, Jane was back in the kitchen cradling her grandson to her. "He's just so beautiful," she whispered with tears in her eyes.

William stood and walked over to stroke the baby's cheek. "He's not going to be much older than his aunt or uncle."

Emily turned her eyes lit with excitement. "You're having a baby, Mama?"

Jane laughed and nodded blushing slightly. "I thought I was too old, but apparently God disagrees with me. I'm due in six months."

"I can't believe I'm going to have a little brother or sister."

Georgie and Abbie stood staring at Jane with awe. "We're getting an aunt or uncle? And he'll be younger than us?" Abbie asked.

William squatted down in front of the girls. "That's right. Is that okay with you?"

Both girls nodded happily. Emily was happy to see how good he was with them. They were staying for a week, and if the girls hadn't liked her mother and stepfather, things would have been harder for her.

Later that evening, her mother slipped her a letter. "Harriett Long asked me to give you this. She and I have formed a friendship."

Emily took the letter and went to her bedroom to read it while she nursed Clarence. "Dear Emily, I'm so happy you've found love through my service. Your mother told me you have a son now. I'm still doing my best to match up young ladies with suitable men out west. I seem to be running out of ladies who need husbands, so if you know of someone, even out there, I'll do my best to broker a marriage for them. I'd love to hear from you when you get a chance, but I understand you're busy with your girls and new baby. I hope to hear from you soon. My best, Harriett."

Emily read the letter once more, and thought back to how frightened she'd been when she'd first knocked on Harriett's door. She hoped soon Harriett would find a love of her own, and not have to spend her time matching up women with men out west to keep herself occupied. She was a lovely woman and deserved the best.

Looking down at her baby suckling at her breast, she knew becoming a mail order bride and finding Benjamin had been the best thing to ever happen to her. She just wished she could share her happiness with the world.

CONTINUE READING for a quick excerpt of *Mail Order Madness*, the next story, a full length novel, in the Brides of Beckham series.

EXCERPT: MAIL ORDER MADNESS

*J*une 1884
        Outside of Beckham, Massachusetts

SUSAN BREATHED a sigh of relief as her day with the neighbor children was finally over. It wasn't that the Jacobs' kids were bad, because her own siblings made them look like angels, but she was just tired of being around children all the time. Everywhere she looked were kids getting into everything. She thought, not for the first time, that she needed to get married and escape everyone else's children. She knew without a doubt, that she could make sure her own kids, if God cursed her with them, behaved well.

She wandered along the dirt road, breathing deeply of the warm summer air. There were flowers in bloom all around her and the trees overhead made a perfect covering protecting her from the hot sun. Summer was her favorite season of the year. She wondered if she'd have time to go for a quick dip in the family's pond after dinner.

She walked the quarter of a mile to her family's farm and went inside, knowing it was time for her to help with dinner. Her sister who was two years younger than her at sixteen had been home with their younger siblings all day, and since there were ten younger siblings, she knew the job would be overwhelming for her sister.

Their mother worked in town for one of the women there cleaning and doing odd jobs around the house. Ever since her youngest brother had broken his arm the previous month, her mother had needed to work to help make ends meet. Their small dairy farm just wasn't enough to support all fourteen of them and pay any doctor bills that came along.

Susan walked through the kitchen and noted the absence of anything cooking. There were egg shells and smashed egg yolks all over the walls and floor. Where was Elizabeth?

She found her in the small parlor with her head in her hands crying. Sitting beside Elizabeth on the sofa, Susan asked, "What'd they do now?"

Elizabeth rubbed her eyes. She was small for her age, and not much bigger than some of their younger brothers. She had the same blond hair and green eyes Susan did, but at that moment, her eyes were red-rimmed and her hair was sticking up in every direction. Susan thought she detected a piece of egg shell in her sister's hair, but didn't say anything about it. "I can*not* do this anymore! They're hellions!" She threw her hands up in the air in defeat.

"Egg fight?" Susan knew there'd been a pretty major egg fight in the kitchen, but that was nothing new in their house. Why would Elizabeth be so upset over something like that?

Elizabeth nodded. "To start with." She took a deep breath. "Have you seen the outhouse? Or been in the barn yet?"

"No…." What had the monsters done this time?

"Well, first they had the egg fight in the kitchen. I walked in and yelled for them to stop before one of the twins beaned me in the side of the head with an egg. I was about to clean it up, but I had to answer nature's call first." Susan nodded, waiting for her sister to get to what the kids had done. "They tipped over the outhouse...with me in it!"

Susan pressed her hand to her mouth to hide the grin that wanted to pop out. It wasn't funny, and she'd be furious if it had been her, but she couldn't help the laughter that was trying to bubble up and out of her. In retrospect the things their siblings did were funny, but it took a while to find enough distance to laugh when you'd been the victim of their mischief.

"Then, when I finally got out and was coming back in the house, I saw Mary's hands were covered with paint. Lavender paint. You know the paint Ma said we could use to paint our room?" Mary was their ten year old sister. She was the next-oldest girl after Elizabeth and the three of them shared a room.

"Yes?"

"Well, she didn't want a purple room, so she used the paint on Mabel."

"Mabel? She actually stood still for that?"

"She wasn't happy. I could hear her mooing from across the yard. Apparently, Mary pulled her in from the field where she was grazing and put her in her stall, before painting her lavender." Elizabeth sighed. "So no pretty room for us. We have to put up with the tic tac toe game on the walls forever."

Susan sighed heavily. "I've got to get out of here. I'm eighteen. I should be married by now and I wouldn't have to put up with this nonsense anymore." She stared off into space for a moment while she thought about it. "Or I guess I could find a job where I could live in. But no kids!"

Elizabeth shook her head. "Then I'd have to deal with them all without you. Ma doesn't much care what they do, and I can't do it alone." Susan's eyes looked fearful at the very idea of Susan leaving her there with the monsters.

"I hate to leave you in this situation by yourself, but honestly? I'm doing it the first chance I get." She looked around. "What happened to the newspaper Pa brought home yesterday?"

"Mary had Mabel stand on it so she wouldn't get paint on the floor of the barn."

That was finally too much for Susan and she felt the laugh rumble up from inside her. "So it's okay to paint the cow, but not to paint the barn floor? Did she get dropped on her *head* when she was a baby?"

"It's not funny! You don't have to stay here with them all day every day. At least you get to go to the Jacobs' farm three days a week. I want to go to the Jacob's farm." Elizabeth's voice was usually calm and serene, but it had deteriorated to a whine.

"We should walk into town together after supper and get a newspaper. Maybe we can find you a job, too." Susan had made up her mind during her conversation with her sister. She was going to get out no matter what she had to do.

"Okay. But what are we going to fix for supper? It'll be time to eat in an hour."

Susan stood up and held her hand out for her sister. "We'll figure something out. And then we'll figure out how to get out of here!"

As they walked into town two hours later, the two sisters talked about their dreams for the future. "I want to be a teacher," Elizabeth admitted. "I don't think I ever want to get married."

Susan grinned. "Just so you don't have to teach our brothers and sisters!" Not getting married was a good idea, in a way, because then she would never be saddled with children, but Susan wanted to find a man to love her.

Elizabeth finally saw the humor in her day and giggled a little. "I want to be a teacher in Oregon. Or California. I hear California is beautiful this time of year." She stopped walking and looked at Susan with fear in her eyes. "You don't think Ma and Pa would ever move to California, do you?"

Susan shook her head, pulling her sister along with her. "That's a better plan." She kicked at a clump of dirt along her path as she walked. They were almost to Beckham. "I really wish I could just get married, but where am I going to meet a man? We go to the same country church we've gone to our whole lives, and the most eligible bachelor is old James Duncan."

Elizabeth wrinkled her nose. "He does seem interested in you." James Duncan was seventy if he was a day, and he'd already buried four wives. He was on the prowl for number five, and Susan seemed to be the object of his affections.

Susan let out a shudder. "I don't think so." They'd reached town and turned to the general store, which was closed, but always set out the "old" newspapers at the end of the day.

Each sister took one, and they settled themselves onto the bench in front of the store to scan the job advertisements. Susan quickly scanned through and stopped at an advertisement for mail order brides. "Mail Order Bride agency needs women who are looking for the adventure of their lives. Men out West need women to marry. Reply in person at 300 Rock Creek Road. See Mrs. Harriett Long."

Elizabeth looked at Susan. "Nothing for me, but did you see the ad for a Mail Order Bride?"

Susan nodded slowly. "I just read it. Am I really desperate enough to get away to answer it, though?" She bit her lip thinking hard about whether that was something she really wanted to do.

"I am! If I wanted to get married and get away from 'the

demon horde' we call brothers and sisters I would do it in a heartbeat."

Susan made up her mind to do it. What could it hurt to just talk to the woman? "Would you go to see Mrs. Long with me?"

Elizabeth looked back down at the paper. "Rock Creek Road. Do you know where that is?"

"I think it's in the rich part of town." Susan's brows drew together. "Why would a rich woman run a mail order bride business?"

"I have no idea." She stood and held her hand out for her sister. "Let's go see if we can find Rock Creek Road."

"You mean it?" Susan had expected Elizabeth to try to talk her out of going, but instead she supported her. She was a good sister.

Elizabeth nodded. "One of us should be able to get out of there!"

Susan took Elizabeth's hand and the two of them walked toward the rich side of town, stopping once to get directions. Once they were in front of the house on Rock Creek Road, Susan's eyes grew wide and she looked at her sister. "This place is huge."

Elizabeth was obviously awestruck. "And beautiful." The two girls stared at the house in awe for a minute.

"How's my hair?" Susan asked.

Elizabeth sighed. "As good as it ever is." They both knew Susan's long blond hair hated to be confined in a bun. There were always tendrils popping out of any hairdo she tried to put it in. There was nothing to do about it now, though. "Let's go up."

"Are you coming in with me?"

"If you want me to."

"Oh, I do! I don't think I could knock on that door without you beside me." Susan wasn't shy, but there was something about the mansion in front of them that intimidated her. She didn't really want to take her sister, but she didn't feel like she could do it alone.

"Let's go then."

The two sisters walked slowly up the sidewalk to the front door. Susan reached out and knocked three times, holding her breath as she waited for someone to come to the door.

It was answered within moments by a tall thin man with dark hair and eyes. "May I help you?"

Susan stared at him for a moment. He seemed to fit in well with the home and she couldn't help but wonder if the owners had bought him as part of it. Elizabeth elbowed her in the side to get her to talk. "I'm here to see Mrs. Long, please."

The man seemed to take them in all at once. His eyes dropped to the newspapers in their hands and he gave a quick nod. "Of course. Mrs. Long is in her office. If you'd come this way?" He led the way toward the back of a long elegant hallway.

Susan wanted to pop her head into every room and see what was behind the closed doors. She'd seen houses like this before, but she'd never been inside one, and she found she wanted to know everything about it.

The man stopped at a door at the end of the hallway, and knocked once, before opening the door. "There are two young ladies here to see you, ma'am."

Susan couldn't see inside the room, but a soft musical voice responded. "Thank you, Higgins. Would you bring some refreshments for us please?"

"Yes, of course." He held the door wide while the two girls found their way in and closed it softly behind them.

Susan looked around the small room they were in. There was a desk with an office chair and a sofa as well as an overstuffed comfortable chair. She felt they were horribly underdressed and wished she had thought to go home and change before they had gone there. She was still wearing the dirty dress she'd watched the children in, and although she'd put her shoes and socks on before leaving the house, she knew her feet were filthy from going barefoot all day even if the pretty lady before her didn't.

Mrs. Long slowly got to her feet and limped the few steps toward the girls. "I'm Harriett Long." When Susan and Elizabeth just stared at her, she smiled and held her hand out. "And you are?"

Susan cleared her throat with embarrassment. "I'm Susan Miller, and this is my sister, Elizabeth. We've come about your advertisement for mail order brides."

Harriett looked between the two sisters. "Have a seat. Are both of you interested in becoming brides?"

Susan shook her head. "No, just me. Elizabeth is just here for moral support." Susan squeezed her sister's hand in silent thanks for going with her.

Harriett smiled as the girls finally sat down on the sofa and she returned to her seat in front of the desk. "Why don't you tell me a little about yourself then, Susan? What makes you interested in becoming a mail order bride?"

"Honestly, it's our home situation."

Harriett's brows drew together quickly. "Are you mistreated by your parents?"

Susan let out a slight laugh. "Oh, no. It's not that at all. In fact, our parents need to find a switch and start using it. Often." She paused for a moment looking at Elizabeth who was grinning at her. "I'm the oldest of twelve children. The oldest four, Elizabeth and I and our two oldest brothers, Michael and Henry, were all strongly disciplined from the beginning. We were raised to take responsibility for our actions. After the four of us, mother just got tired, I think."

"How so?" Harriett's eyes were on Susan's and she was taking in every word the younger woman said. It was as if Susan were imparting important knowledge.

"Well, our younger siblings are...." She didn't want to use the word hellions, but that and "demon horde" were the only words that came to mind. She bit her lip for a moment.

"Satan's spawn." The words, loud and clear and unashamed, came from Elizabeth.

Harriett choked back a laugh. "That bad?" She picked up the cup of tea Higgins had brought to them and took a sip.

Susan nodded emphatically. "Worse. Anyway, I've got to get out of there. My one stipulation for a husband is he must not have any children. If God curses me with children of my own, I'll raise them with a strict hand and a long switch." She needed to get that out of the way to begin with. She was not going to raise some man's problems.

Harriett smiled, obviously delighted by the honesty of the young women sitting in front of her. "How old are you, Susan? I won't send out a woman younger than eighteen."

"I was eighteen in March."

"Well, let's see then." Harriett turned to her desk and flipped through the different letters there. "No, he has children," she mumbled. She finally found a letter halfway through her stack and read through it quickly. "He's the one I was looking for. I think Jesse Dailey is just the man you're looking for." She handed the letter to Susan for her to read.

Susan opened the letter and held it to where Elizabeth could read it along with her. It struck her that as much as she wanted to get away from 'the demon horde' she would miss Elizabeth just as much. Elizabeth had always been more than a sister. She was her best friend. She made a silent vow to tell her so before she left.

"Dear potential bride, My name is Jesse Dailey and I'm a newspaperman in Fort Worth, Texas. I hope to be able to buy a ranch in the area soon, so I'm looking for a bride who is willing to save every penny to help me toward that goal. I'm not sure what to tell you about myself, so I'm just going to ramble for a bit. I'm tall with dark hair and brown eyes. I've lived in Texas my entire life, and grew up on a ranch here. I enjoy quiet walks in the country and reading. I go to church every Sunday. I'm well-respected in town as a hard-hitting newspaperman who makes sure he always tells the truth, even if it's not what people want to hear. I'm twenty-three years old and have never married. I enjoy a good home cooked meal, and would request my bride be able to cook. I'd like someone between the ages of eighteen and twenty-two. I'm looking forward to getting married and settling down. All the best, Jesse."

Susan smiled as she read he wanted someone who could cook. She'd been cooking for years and knew there would be no trouble there. She certainly matched his requests. She looked up at Harriett. "I'll take him."

Harriett laughed. "He's not just a man on the shelf that you can choose. You need to write him back and we'll go from there." She handed Susan a pen, ink and paper. "Go ahead and write the letter now. All correspondence needs to go through me."

Susan took the pen and dipped it into the ink well. What to write? After a moment of thinking, she put the pen to paper. "Dear Jesse, My name is Susan Miller. I live on a small farm outside of Beckham, Massachusetts with my parents and my eleven younger brothers and sisters. I'm eighteen years old and I'm a good cook. I'd love to cook for just two people instead of fourteen. I also enjoy long walks through the country and reading books, although I rarely have free time to do either one. I do not mind living frugally, because it's the only way I know. I am of medium height and have blond hair and green eyes. I've never been to Texas, but I've read about it some, and find it fascinating. I'd love to move there to be your bride." Susan set the pen down and read the letter aloud, making sure Mrs. Long approved of what she'd written.

Harriett nodded. "That's perfect. Sign it, and I'll send it off with the morning's mail."

Susan quickly signed her name to the bottom and handed the unfolded paper to the older woman. "Now what?"

"Come see me in about a month to see what he says. If he decides you're the one he wants, he'll send you some money for the trip to Texas, and a train ticket."

"Sounds good." Susan stood up, realizing she hadn't touched the tea and cookies Higgins had brought in while she was working on her letter. She grabbed a cookie from the plate. "Thank you so much." She held her hand out to Mrs. Long. "I'll see you in about a month, I guess."

Harriett got to her feet slowly. "I look forward to it." She smiled at Elizabeth. "It was nice meeting you, Elizabeth." She walked the two sisters to the front door and watched them walk away, smiling to herself.

~

ONE MONTH LATER, Susan knocked on Harriett's door. She'd had to sneak away from the farm to come into town, because her younger siblings would have begged to come with her. She could just imagine the mischief they would get into in a house like Mrs. Long's. *There would be nothing left but rubble,* she thought.

Higgins answered the door promptly. "Come right in." He opened the door wide and led her to the office again. He knocked once and opened the office door. "Miss Miller is here to see you, Ma'am. I'll get some refreshments." He closed the door softly behind him.

Harriett got to her feet and smiled as Susan walked in. Susan couldn't help but wonder what had happened to the older woman to make her move so slowly. She obviously had an injured leg, but how had it been injured? She'd been taught not to ask such things, but she certainly wanted to.

Harriett waved to the sofa. "Have a seat. Your letter came just this morning, so this is good timing." Once Susan was seated, Harriett handed her the letter. "I didn't open it, because it's addressed to you." She turned away to look through some papers on her desk and to give Susan a bit of privacy with her letter.

Susan took a deep breath before opening the letter. She desperately wanted there to be a train ticket inside. As soon as she opened it, a train ticket, a check and some cash fell out. She smiled, knowing he wanted her. She picked up the check, which was made out to Mrs. Harriett Long, and handed it to her. She picked up the cash and showed Harriett. "Is this for me to keep?"

Harriett nodded. "It's for any expenses you may have. Your train ride will be a long one, so you'll want to keep at least half of that for food on the train. The rest you can use for clothes or anything else you may need." She paused for a moment. "What's the date on the ticket?"

Susan looked down to check. "I leave July twenty eighth. That's a Monday, right?"

Harriett checked her calendar. "It is. That gives you ten days. Do you think you can get clothes made in time?"

Susan thought about it. "If Elizabeth and I ignore all the kids, we can probably get a couple of dresses made. Do I need a formal wedding dress?"

"I usually say 'yes' to that. See if he mentioned the wedding in his letter." Harriett indicated the letter in the younger woman's hand.

Susan looked down and laughed at herself. She'd been so

excited about the train ticket she hadn't bothered to read the letter. "I guess I should read it, shouldn't I?"

Harriett grinned. "I know you're excited to get away, so I won't say anything."

"Dear Susan, I'm so excited you answered my letter. You sound like you're going to fill the missing space in my life perfectly. I've enclosed a train ticket for Monday, July twenty eighth. I will be waiting for you at the train station in Fort Worth on Wednesday, August sixth. I'll carry a sign with your name on it, so you'll know immediately who I am. I'm not going to subject you to a big wedding after your long trip, so I will arrange for us to marry at the courthouse with just my brother and his children present. I hope that meets with your approval. If it's a problem, you can let me know when you get here, and we'll make other arrangements. I can't wait to meet you. Yours, Jesse."

"He said we'd just marry at the courthouse. I think I'll just make a new Sunday dress. That's better than spending a lot of money on a gown I'll only wear one time."

Harriett nodded. "May I read the letter?"

Susan didn't feel any real attachment for Jesse, and he hadn't put anything private in the letter, so she readily agreed, handing it to Harriett.

Susan studied the older woman while her head was bowed reading the letter. If you ignored their dress, Harriett could have been her sister. She looked to be around twenty-eight and had blond hair and green eyes. She was slim and seemed very graceful despite her pronounced limp.

"Everything looks good here. The train ride is a long one. You're not going to have a chance to bathe or anything once you're on the train. That's one of the biggest complaints of my brides. Will that bother you?"

Susan made a face. She didn't like the idea of going for over a week without a bath, but it would be worth it to get married and away from her family once and for all. "I'll manage."

"Most men do make some kind of arrangement for you to bathe before your wedding, I've found."

"Good. I can't imagine getting married without at least bathing first." The idea of a long train ride was both exciting and daunting.

"I can't imagine that either." Harriett studied the younger woman for a moment. "Would you like me to see you off? I do that for most of the brides I send out."

Susan thought about that for a few seconds. "I think that would be good. I'm sure Elizabeth will be there if she can, but I have no way of knowing whether she'll be able to get away or not."

"What time does your train leave on Wednesday?"

"Eight in the morning."

"Come by here at seven and we'll walk to the train station together. We can talk on the way. If your sister comes, great. Then there will be two of us to see you off."

Harriett stood and led Susan to the door. On impulse, Susan turned and hugged Harriett before leaving. "Thank you so much. You've helped me a lot."

"It's my job to help as much as I can. I think of each of my brides as a friend."

Susan thought about Harriett's words as she walked to the general store just a few streets over. Beckham wasn't a large city, so nothing was very far apart.

Once she got to the store, she went inside, looking at fabrics for some new dresses. Everything she owned had once belonged to her mother and had been cut down for her. Jesse had been generous with the money he'd sent, and although she knew she needed some for the trip, she could buy enough fabric for three or four dresses without a problem.

She flipped through the bolts of cloth and picked out a pink with small flowers, a blue check, a pretty lavender, which she realized matched the cow exactly, and a forest green to match her eyes. She also bought an entire bolt of white linen for new undergarments. She couldn't wait to get home to start sewing.

After paying for her purchases, she carried the small wooden box the shopkeeper had given her home. Her mind was full of how perfect life would be without poorly behaved children climbing all over her. Oh, she had no illusions. She knew someday she'd have children too. Her mother had twelve for goodness sakes! But she would have some time before the children arrived to just be Susan. She loved the idea of just taking care of laundry and cooking and cleaning for two people. She sighed. Life would be heavenly.

~

JULY 1884
Outside of Fort Worth, Texas

JESSE DAILEY TOOK a gulp of his water as he watched his four young nephews run around his brother's house screaming. The four of them had been causing his brother problems ever since his sister-in-law, Caroline, had died at the birth of two year old twins, Thomas and Walter. He shook his head at his brother wondering just how he could live amidst the chaos. "I have news."

David raised his eyebrow waiting. "You found a ranch?"

Jesse shook his head. "Not yet, but I'm saving every penny." He folded his hands behind his head and leaned back in the kitchen chair. He'd just had a good meal, thanks to his brother's cook and housekeeper, Sadie. "I'm getting married."

David's jaw dropped. "Married! I didn't even know you were courting anyone."

Jesse grinned. "I don't have time to court anyone. Not with spending every waking moment at the newspaper office, picking up extra articles so I can make enough to buy a ranch. I like being a reporter, but my heart is in ranching. I should have been the big brother."

David laughed. "I've told you a hundred times, you're welcome to half the ranch. You can even live here with the boys and me while you build yourself a house." He kicked his brother's foot affectionately. "Who's the girl?" He reached for a cookie and popped half of it into his mouth.

"I sent for a mail order bride." Jesse said the words nonchalantly, knowing they'd surprise his brother.

David choked on his cookie. After a moment, his eyes watering, he asked, "Seriously?"

"Seriously. She's going to be here in a couple of weeks. You coming to the wedding? I'm just going to do a courthouse thing. No need for a big church wedding when she doesn't know anyone here."

"Of course, I'll be there. Girl got a name?" David studied his younger brother as if he was trying to decide if he'd lost his mind.

Jesse's brow furrowed. "Susan." He thought over the details of her letter. "She's 18 and the oldest of twelve kids. Says she can cook. I think she's just ready to get out of Massachusetts."

David nodded. "I'll watch and see how it works out for you, and I may do the same." He jerked his thumb over his shoulder to where his older two boys were pointing imaginary guns at each other and screaming and his two youngest were pushing each other. "I'll never get a bride who knows me and my brood. I need one who is unsuspecting."

Jesse laughed and clapped his brother on the shoulder. "You have a point."

David sighed. "Sure would be nice to have a warm body in bed at night again, though. A man gets lonely."

"I thought you were going to court that sweet nanny of yours." He looked around, realizing she wasn't there. "Where is she anyway?"

"Where do you think? After the boys put a toad in her bed for the third time this week, she left. She said, 'I'm not going to stay here another minute with your boys. They're monsters.' Then she stuck a finger in my face and told me if I didn't find a good woman to be their mother and take them in hand, they'd be ruined forever." He shrugged. "I guess she wasn't volunteering to be that good woman."

Jesse shook his head, sympathizing. David had dealt with the four boys on his own for a year, before deciding to find himself a wife. He hadn't felt right about remarrying before that. By that time the boys had been running wild for too long, and their behavior showed it. "Maybe a mail order bride is something you need to do. Next time I see you, I'll give you the address of the woman in Massachusetts that runs the agency I used." He stood up. "I've got to go. I promised my editor I'd run to Hell's Half Acre tonight to do a story on a man who was murdered there."

David made a face. "Be careful. The Acre gets worse every year. Do you have anyone who can go with you?"

Jesse shrugged. "I was going to ask you, but you seem to be without a nanny for the boys." Again.

"Yeah, I'd go, but it's not a good time. Find someone, though. You really shouldn't go there alone. Especially at night." He looked out the window. It was dusk, but by the time Jesse made it back to town it would be full night. "Be really careful whether someone's with you or not." He made a face. "Maybe you should wait until daylight."

"I'll be okay, big brother. I've been taking care of myself for several years now."

David stood up and hugged his brother. "Take care."

Jesse yelled over the din, "Goodbye monster children! I'll be back!"

Albert and Lewis looked up from their game of cowboys and Indians and ran over to hug their uncle. "See you at church!"

The two younger boys ignored him as usual. With a last wave, he left, riding into town to find out what had happened to Joshua Campbell, a man who had died there the previous evening. He didn't have time to find someone to go with him, so he went alone. He'd be okay. He'd been in The Acre for stories lots of times. Just never at night.

To SIGN up for Kirsten Osbourne's mailing list and receive notice of new titles as they are available, click here.

Kirsten's Complete Collection

ALSO BY

Sign up for instant notification of all of Kirsten's New Releases Text 'BOB' to 42828

And

For a complete list of Kirsten's works head to her website wwww.kirstenandmorganna.com

ABOUT THE AUTHOR

www.kirstenandmorganna.com